Another Dreadful Fairy Book

Another Dreadful Fairy Book

NARRATED BY
Quentin Q. Quacksworth, Esq.

WRITTEN BY
Jon Etter

WITH ILLUSTRATIONS BY
Adam Horsepool

AMBERJACK
PUBLISHING

CHICAGO

AMBERJACK
PUBLISHING

Amberjack Publishing
An imprint of Chicago Review Press Incorporated
814 North Franklin Street
Chicago, Illinois 60610

10 9 8 7 6 5 4 3 2 1

CIP data for this book is available from the Library of Congress.

ISBN: 978-1-948705-62-2
E-ISBN: 978-1-948705-63-9

"Libraries are about Freedom. Freedom to read, freedom of ideas, freedom of communication. They are about education (which is not a process that finishes the day we leave school or university), about entertainment, about making safe spaces, and about access to information."
—Neil Gaiman, "Why Our Future Depends on Libraries, Reading and Daydreaming"

FROM JON:

To my parents, Stan and Connie Etter, for reading to me and countless other acts of love, and Forrest Public Library, for letting me grow up in its stacks.

FROM QUACKSWORTH:

To my dear, darling family for their kindness and comfort as I slogged through this odious assignment: my splendid spouse, Quintessa, and my precious, precocious progeny, Quentin, Jr., Quigley, Quinn, Quentin III, Quimbey, Quentin IV, Quella, Quinten, and Becky.

· PREFACE ·

An Admonition from the Narrator

Let me begin, dear Reader, by telling you how terribly you have disappointed me.

At the beginning of Mr. Etter's previous fairy book, which focused on the adventures of the cranky sprite Shade, the crooked brownie Ginch, and the just plain silly pixie the Professor as they found their way to the most wondrous Grand Library of Elfame, I warned you that it was a truly dreadful tale filled with disappointingly contrary fairies and urged you to move on to more proper and morally improving tales. And knowing what an intelligent and thoughtful reader you were, I had little doubt that you would put down the dratted thing and read neither a jot nor a tittle more. But did you heed my warnings? Did you put down that horrendous book that I was contractually obligated—much to my chagrin!—to narrate and pick up one of the wonderful books that I am actually proud to have worked on, like *Lovey Tumkins and the Pleasant and Helpful Wee Folk* or *Honest Jim and the Do-Right Lads*?

Sadly, we both know you did not. Instead, you read that dreadful book cover to cover and even urged friends to read it, doing who knows how much damage to the moral character of all involved including, I fear, *me*. Why, after narrating that terribly improper book, I actually began to wonder how important it truly is not to mix up one's fruit salad fork with one's leafy green salad fork at dinner, and if perhaps *Honest Jim* might not be a tish more interesting if Jim were to get up to a little mischief at some point (the correct answers being, of course, horribly important and perish the thought!). And all because *you* refused to follow the advice of your elders. Dreadful, not-so-good Reader! Truly dreadful!

Since appealing to your decency and good taste has clearly failed, I feel a different approach is now in order, for all of our sakes. I warn you: Do not read this book! If you do, I shall be forced to report your actions to your parents, your teachers, local law enforcement, and your dear, sweet aunt Agnes. And once I have done that, I sincerely doubt you will receive any of Aunt Agnes's delightful hand-knit socks for your birthday this year. Just think about that before turning this page: *no hand-knit birthday socks!*

There! I am sorry to issue such threats, but enough is enough. Now I have a dreadful tale to narrate that you under no circumstances should read, lest you encourage the author to write more tales such as this one and possibly lead us all down the road to moral ruin. Sweet St. Figgymigg help us if that happens!

And so I remain,

Your Reluctant Narrator,

Quentin Q. Quacksworth, Esq.

UNITED FEDERATION OF NARRATORS, RACONTEURS, ANECDOTISTS, AND GENERAL TELLERS OF TALES, LOCAL 42

In which one of Shade's least
favorite people pops in for a visit . . .

S hade closed the door to her room high inside the
immense magical oak tree that housed Elfame's
Grand Library, walked to the railing, and looked
down. Hundreds of feet below, the wood floor showed
thousands of years of growth rings on top of which sat
tables, study nooks, and one large wooden desk. Shade
smiled . . . then dived over the rail.

She opened her gray, brown, yellow, and black butterfly wings—which, when fully open, looked a lot like the face of an owl—and began to glide downward in lazy circles, following the spiraling path that took visitors to every level of the great library tree. Along the path, the walls were lined with books, their leather and cloth covers all the colors in the world. Shade's heart was still filled with joy at the sight, even after she had lived and worked in the Grand Library for over six months. She closed her eyes for a moment and inhaled, savoring the musty smell of old books.

"Could life ever get better than this?" Shade murmured.

"Oi! Flutterbutt! Stop muckin' about!" a bulldog-headed fairy wearing a bowler hat and pinstriped, double-breasted vest shouted.

"Okay, maybe it could get a little better," Shade muttered to herself. "Go chase your tail, Fleabag! I'm getting there!"

"Bloody sproites," she heard Caxton mutter, although she could see the smile on his jowly face.

Shade circled down another hundred feet and then alighted in front of the maple desk that sat in the middle of the great main reading room. Behind the desk sat a black cat in a cream-colored shirt and brown vest who looked up over the top of his reading glasses at Shade. "*Guten Morgen, Fraulein Shade!*" he said cheerfully.

"Good morning, Johannes," Shade replied. "Where should I start today?"

"Vy don't you open the doors, then I have the very exciting discovery to share vith you."

"Really? What is it?"

"First, you let in the patrons, ja?"

"Fine, fine," Shade said as she walked over to the first of ten doors that opened identical doors hidden in the sides of ten identical trees growing in different parts of Elfame, the magical land of the fairies. I know, good Reader: Ten different trees in ten different places that all lead to the same space that exists in all ten locations and separate from them at the same time is a terribly confusing concept. I'm afraid that to make sense of it, one would need to know an awful lot about both dimensional magic and extra- and intra-spatial engineering, neither of which, regrettably, were covered during my studies in narrating school. No doubt one of your exceedingly clever parents can explain it to you. But to get back to our story, Shade flipped the latch on the door labeled "Meadowbrook" and pulled open the door to allow the sun of the pleasant meadow beyond to shine momentarily on her chestnut brown face and a cool spring breeze to blow through her curly black hair.

Shade sighed happily, then proceeded to the door to Dinas Ffaraon, the home of the Seelie Court, the longtime rulers of Elfame. On the other side, waiting patiently for it to open, as she did most days, was a young elf, hardly older than fifty seasons, her pale face barely peeking out from the hood of the green cloak she had worn on every visit to the Grand Library. "Good morning," Shade said. The child nodded politely on her way to the nearest section of bookshelves.

Next Shade went to the door to Ande-Dubnos, the home of the Sluagh Horde, the longtime enemies of the Seelie Court who now controlled roughly half of the fairy lands thanks to an uneasy truce established after the last great war. Another elf, the same age as the last and similarly attired but with a black cloak and dark skin, waited eagerly. When greeted, he paused long enough to smile and return her greeting before rushing off to the stacks.

Shade unlocked door after door until she came to the last one: the door to her childhood home of Pleasant Hollow. She frowned. Her frown deepened when she heard an insistent pounding coming from the other side. Quite certain she knew who was there, Shade rolled her eyes and opened the door. The vivid orange hand that had been knocking connected sharply with Shade's forehead.

"Ow! Watch what you're dingle-dangle doing!" Shade cried, using exactly the sort of dreadfully rude language—two of the rudest swear words of the fairies, no less—that makes this book so utterly inappropriate for you, dear Reader.

Sungleam Flutterglide, chieftainess of the sprites of

Pleasant Hollow, looked down her nose at Shade. "I see that your time around all these . . . *books* . . . "—Chieftainess Flutterglide looked like she swallowed a bug when she said the word—"hasn't improved your mood or your manners, Lillyshadow Glitterdemalion."

"Not when I have to deal with clodheads, Flutterbutt," Shade retorted.

"That's *Chieftainess Sungleam Flutterglide*, Lillyshadow, and you know it."

"It's 'Flutterbutt' until you start calling me 'Shade,' Flutterbutt," Shade said, crossing her arms. "So what can we help you with today? St. Whitman the Wise's *Blades of Barley*? *The Crimson Character* by Nathaniel Thornapple? Maybe—"

"You know I want nothing of the sort. I want this . . . this . . . " Chieftainess Flutterglide searched for the word. Failing to come up with it, she gestured frantically all around.

Shade smirked. "Library?"

Chieftainess Flutterglide pointed her finger at Shade's face. "Yes, *library*," she said, her voice dripping with contempt. "I want this *library* out of Pleasant Hollow."

"And what exactly is the problem with it?"

"First of all, all sorts of new fairies are coming to our village to visit this place all the time now. *Different* fairies."

"Yeah, I noticed them coming through the door to the library lately. It's great."

"It most certainly is not! Pleasant Hollow is a community of and for sprites, as you well know, and we believe it best if fairies stay with their own kind," Chieftainess Flutterglide returned stiffly.

"And that's why I don't live there anymore." Shade frowned. "Well, that and because you clodheads burned my house down. So, have anything else profoundly ignorant to share?"

"I absolutely do! In addition to the . . . *unsavory* element that this *library* has brought to our beloved Pleasant Hollow, it has caused some sprites of the village, including some of our children—*our children*—to question the wisdom of the decisions made by the village elders and myself."

Shade's smirk turned into an actual smile. "Really? Huh. Maybe there's hope for all of you yet."

"Now see here, *Lillyshadow Glitterdemalion*—it is bad enough that you and your parents and grandparents and great-grandparents have been thorns in the side of authority for four generations, but now other people are asking questions and suggesting that we do things differently. *Differently!*"

A chorus of shushes sprang from the many visitors who had entered the library during her tirade.

"Sounds like a very promising development," Shade said dismissively. "Now if you'll—"

"Oh, it is *not*. Especially when it's coming from—" Chieftainess Flutterglide stopped abruptly and jabbed an accusing finger toward a chubby gray sprite and a thin, moss-colored one who had just come through the Pleasant Hollow doorway. "Right there! Exactly what I'm talking about. Those two are *children* and here they are: reading books and getting big ideas—"

"Which is exactly why I am here," a deep, haughty voice rumbled.

2

*In which a bugbear bugs Shade,
the head librarians, and even me,
your humble Narrator . . .*

Shade turned to see who had spoken. Striding toward her came what looked like a bear—a long, lean, hungry, vicious-looking one with brownish-red fur the color of dried blood, except his face, which was going white with age, giving it an almost skull-like look. No Teddy or Winnie he, for he was a *bugbear*, one of the most ill-tempered and vicious of all fairies. This one was clad in a black suit and greatcoat with a stiff white collar and a circular, wide-brimmed hat sitting atop his head. Poking out of the elbows of his outfit were two wicked, barbed spikes like the stingers of bees, and perched on his grizzled muzzle was a pair of glasses with smoked lenses, hiding his eyes from view. The bugbear looked down at Shade, gave a dismissive snort, and gazed around the library. "I must speak with the head librarians!" he declared loudly.

A gray, monkey-faced gargoyle dressed in a blue satin jacket and knee-pants strode over. Atop his head perched a curly white wig and clutched in one hand was a china coffee cup. Not so much walking as gliding next to him was a thin, elegant woman with long hair and a flowing gown, every inch of her body made of brilliant white marble.

"I'm sorry, but we must ask zat you keep your voice down," the gargoyle, François Marie, said. "Zis is a place of study and contemplation."

"And how may we be of assistance?" Émilie, the

stone woman, asked politely, but with a hint of annoyance in her marble-smooth voice.

"I am Grand Scrutinizer Norwell Drabbury, head of the newly formed Ministry of Ordinariness, Averageness, and Normalcy. I am duly authorized by both the Seelie and Sluagh courts to seek out and . . . " Drabbury sneered, exposing sharp, yellow fangs, " . . . *attend to* any threats to either court, the established peace, and the physical, mental, and moral health of all parts and residents of the land. And M.O.A.N. has determined that this place is most clearly a *threat*."

"What?" Shade asked, stunned. "That is one of the dumbest things I've ever heard. And that's saying something since I grew up in Pleasant Hollow."

"Just as I have always said!" Chieftainess Flutterglide crowed. "For four generations your family have been nothing but ill-mannered troublemakers, and it's all been because of those horrid *books* you've kept your noses buried in."

"I'm sure you're quite right, milady," Drabbury agreed, shaking his head in sorrow. "And troublemaking, bad manners, disrespect for authority figures—these and so many other problems—will no doubt spread throughout the land unless something is done about this library."

The foreheads of Émilie and François furrowed; their eyes narrowed. "And what exactly do you propose to do about it?" Émilie asked.

"Well, we at M.O.A.N. hope that *we* won't have to do anything and that we can count on your wisdom and good sense to do what is right. For one thing, you can begin by restricting access to this library to members of the Seelie and Sluagh courts and authorized scholars and dignitaries. All others, especially impressionable children, are to be banned. As we know, reading has a tendency to lead to questions, and society works best with strict obedience to authority. Questions cause problems."

"*Oui*—ze *best* questions always cause problems for zose 'oo *should* 'ave problems," François replied.

"We absolutely refuse," Émilie said, her usually melodious voice now sounding like flint sparking against flint.

"In fact, we're adding a children's section to the library specifically to encourage kids to come in here and read," Shade said, pointedly. It was an idea she had considered for a while and now seemed an ideal time to mention it. François and Émilie turned to her, puzzled. Behind them, Shade noticed that the two cloaked young elves who had come in earlier were also looking at her and seemed rather pleased.

"*Oui!* That we are," declared Émilie. François gave Shade a wink and a nod.

"We shall see about that," Drabbury growled. He reached into his coat and drew out a large sheaf of papers that he held out to François. "In the meantime, M.O.A.N. has determined that the following books in your collection are filled with troubling content and are likely to corrupt readers. I insist they be handed over this instant for removal and disposal."

"What? Let me see this!" Shade cried, grabbing the sheets from Drabbury's sharp claws. Books so terrible that nobody should be allowed to read them? The idea seemed ridiculous. "*The Adventures of Hagan Finnegan?* That's a great book!"

"Utterly inappropriate for young readers. It uses and encourages the use of foul language," Drabbury replied coolly.

"Oh, puckernuts to that!" Shade replied. "*Fuzzy Tinker and the Wizard's Rock*?"

"He engages in conjuration while still a minor and is rude and disobedient to authority figures."

"Yeah, because some of them are stupid and evil, you mudbrain!" It felt like Shade's blood was about to boil. "*The Fairy Godfather*? *The Snatcher in the Barley*? *An Expedition to the Underground World*? What could you possibly—"

Drabbury snatched back his list. "I am a very busy fairy and do not have time to explain my actions to impertinent young sprites. In the name of M.OA.N. and for the good of all fairies, I demand you hand over every copy of every title listed on these pages," Drabbury growled, thrusting the papers at François.

Everyone in the room—Shade, Émilie, Flutterglide, Johannes, and the many visitors—looked at François. He calmly handed his coffee cup to Émilie, took the papers from Drabbury, smiled, and tore them in half.

"'Ere," he said, shoving them back at the bugbear. "As ze good junior librarian Shade would say, get dingled and dangled."

"And donkled." Shade smirked. "Especially donkled."

"Feel free to use any door you choose to leave," Émilie said. "So long as you do *leave*."

Drabbury stuffed the torn papers in his cloak. A dull red light glowed through the dark lenses of his glasses. "This is far from over," he said, his voice the low rumble of thunder in the distance. "And all of you will sorely regret your impudence when I return."

"Doubt it," Shade replied. She turned to Chieftainess Flutterglide. "You can leave too, saphead."

"I will, but mark my words, I will not rest until your library is out of my village!" Chieftainess Flutterglide declared.

"Come, Chieftainess, I believe we have much to discuss," the bugbear said. The two stormed out, slamming the door behind them.

Now before I recount Johannes's wondrous discovery that sends Shade off on the adventure of a lifetime,

I feel I must address the elephant in the room. By this I mean something that may be troubling you that you, kind Reader, are far too polite to bring up even though it looms here between us, and I do not mean Yoshini, our beloved family elephant. She, of course, would not be allowed here in my study as I narrate this. As a point of fact, she has only ever been in the house the one time, when my dear daughter Quella sneaked her in during a sleepover, and she (Yoshini, not Quella) made quite a mess of the solarium and stripped half the plants in the arboretum of their foliage before settling in for a nap in the grand hall. Never again.

No, the proverbial (as opposed to literal) elephant in the room is Grand Scrutinizer Norwell Drabbury's insistence on the removal of books that he deems "corrupting" and "inappropriate" from the Grand Library of Elfame. Given my objections to you reading this and Mr. Etter's previous terrible tome, you might very well assume that I agree with Mr. Drabbury's demands. You assume wrong. While I definitely do not believe you should be reading this book, and while I do believe that these dreadful fairy books are in no way morally improving, I *do* believe that the choice to read them or not—and I do so wish you had chosen "*not*"—should be up to you and you alone, as should be the case with most books and readers.

So there you have it. As the saying goes, when you assume, you . . . very likely will reach the wrong conclusion. Or something to that effect. I don't recall the exact saying at the moment. Well, no matter—we have a dreadful tale to continue.

3

*In which we learn there is more to
Radishbottom than meets the eye . . .*

"Dewey! Caxton!" François shouted as he
and Émilie headed up the ramp. "To our
office! We must 'ave ze reorganization and
create ze section for children, *allons y*!"

Shade heard a little squeal of joy just before a
brownie with a pointy beard in a brown three-piece
suit raced out of the stacks on the main floor and up

the ramp after the head librarians. There was nothing Dewey, their collections chief, loved more than a good reorganization. With a heavy sigh and muttering several rude words, Caxton trudged behind them.

While excited to create a children's section, Shade was infuriated by Chieftainess Flutterglide and the bugbear. "And the day just started," Shade said. "What more could happen?"

Actually, a good deal more can happen over the course of a day, as you well know, kind Reader. For example, yesterday between my morning toast and tea and my afternoon toast and tea, approximately forty-seven and a half things occurred in my life. Which, now that I think of it, is exactly the same number of things that occurred during that time on the previous day. And the day before that. And the day before that ... Hmm ... I'll have to mull that over later, but getting back to my original point, an awful lot can happen during the day, and you, being such an astute and knowledgeable Reader, no doubt expect that more *will* happen to Shade. And while this story may disappoint you on many other levels, it will not on this particular point.

Shade felt a soft tap on her shoulder. Johannes stood there, a smile on his muzzle and a twinkle in his green cat eyes. "Please to come vith me, Fraulein Shade, for I have made a most vonderful discovery."

Johannes led Shade to a room that branched off the central spiral. It had no windows and was instead lit by wall sconces shaped like fireflies, their wings spread and magical fires burning within their glass tails. Filling the room were tables covered in books. Some were missing covers, some had broken spines, some were charred by fire, some were warped and stained by water—all were in need of repair. In her six months living in the Grand Library, Shade had never seen this room before. "Is this where you fix up the books?"

"Ja, and this is vere I make my discovery." Johannes picked up a book from a nearby table.

Shade instantly recognized the blue leather-bound book, the only one that had survived the fire that had robbed her of her Pleasant Hollow home. As a child, it had taught her about all the places in Elfame that she had never seen, and six months ago its sometimes accurate guidance had helped her find her way to her current home. "It's my copy of Radishbottom's *Traveling in the Greater Kingdom*," she said. "I donated that to the library when I came here."

"Ja, vell, since ve already have copies of it, ve thought ve make of it the gift back to you, but first I fix it up a little. The library gets busy and so only now do I have time to vork on it. And ven I do, I make the discovery. Vatch!"

Johannes placed the book on a table covered with jars, knives, needles, brushes, spools of thread, and other tools for book repair. He unscrewed a jar, took out a pinch of powder, and sprinkled it on Shade's book. At first, nothing happened, but after a moment the book began to glow.

"What's happening?" Shade asked. "What does it mean?"

"It means this," Johannes said. He picked up a knife and stabbed at the book.

"No! Stop!" Shade shouted. She watched in horror as the knife plunged toward the book cover . . . and then in amazement when the blade snapped.

Johannes held up the handle of the broken knife and chuckled. "You see, the book is—ow!" He rubbed the shoulder Shade had just slugged. "For vy do you hit me?"

"For making me think you were going to destroy my book, fuzzball," Shade said, picking up the book, which still glowed with faint blue light. She held it protectively to her chest.

"I vas trying to be dramatic."

"Well, don't."

"From now on, I most definitely vill not. Now, if I am not to be hit again, I vill finish vhat I vas saying: Your book has the protection spell on it."

"But it was damaged in the fire," Shade said, turning it over in her hands, looking at the charred edges and slightly water-warped pages.

"Only a little vhen all of your other books burn up," Johannes explained. "It is the very subtle magic—the spell allows the minor damage but not the major so most vould never know the spell exists. I almost didn't find it myself, and I am very good at the book magic."

Shade was confused. "So someone put a magical spell on this book to protect it?"

"Ja."

"But why not do it for all the books we owned?" Shade thought of all the books she had grown up with that were now gone forever, books she had spent her entire life reading or having read to her as she sat on the laps of her father and mother. Books that had felt like part of her family. Even part of her. "And why this one of all the books we had? My father barely ever looked at it."

"That I do not know, but perhaps ve vill find out because of the other discovery I have made," Johannes said, picking up a pair of tweezers.

Johannes opened the book until the cover was at a perfect 90 degree angle, then pointed the tweezers to the spine. "You vill see that when the cover is open to this exact point, there is the smallest gap. And in the gap," at this point, Johannes paused, carefully inserted the tweezers into the gap, and slowly pulled out a folded piece of paper, "is maybe the hidden message, ja? And there is another in the other end."

Johannes extracted another piece of paper from the other end of the spine and placed it next to the first. Shade looked down at them, dumbfounded. "What are those?" she asked. "Have they been in there my whole life?"

Johannes shrugged. "I do not know. I thought it best to leave them vhere they vere until I could show you. Shall ve see vhat they are?"

Shade nodded. "You take that one and I'll take this one."

She picked up the piece of paper nearest her and began to unfold the thin sheet. It read:

25-10, 1-70, 310-2, 29-157, 47-42, 211-198, 68-9, 18-98, 151-58, 83-1, 261-111, 3-88, 50-10, 187-138, 19-6

"It's a bunch of numbers," Shade said. "What's on yours?"

Johannes shook his head. "Nothing."

"Nothing? What do you mean, 'nothing'?"

"It is the blank sheet," Johannes said, holding up the unfolded paper.

"Why would anyone go to the trouble of hiding a blank sheet like that? That doesn't make any sense." Shade snatched the paper from Johannes's hand and glared at it as if looking at the paper hard enough would make words miraculously appear there, just as you have tried to do when you've been assigned essays by your teacher about what you did on summer vacation, what you want to be if you grow up, which Victorian essayist you would most want to have tea with (other than Matthew Arnold because, as your teacher pointed out, every child wishes they could have tea with Matthew Arnold), and such.

However, unlike your attempts to make words appear on a blank page by staring at it, Shade's were successful.

4

In which our plot really gets rolling . . .

As Shade stared, words written in her father's hand slowly appeared.

"More bibliomancy! The letter that only the intended recipient can read!" Johannes gasped.

"But my dad didn't know any magic," Shade said.

"Apparently, he did," Johannes replied. "Vhy, ve have right here so far examples of two of the six types of bibliomancy. First, ve have . . . "

But Johannes's enthusiastic explanation of book magic fell on deaf ears as Shade read the words written by her late father whom she missed so much:

Dear Shade,

If you're reading this, then I must be gone. However it happened, I am so sorry to leave you there alone—first your mother in that horrible war and now me—but I know that you will be fine. You've grown into such a clever sprite, more than capable of taking care of herself.

When I felt you were old enough, I planned on revealing this great family secret: I, like my father and his father before him, am part of a secret society. Long ago, in the center of Elfame stood a great library—the Great Library—until dark forces sacked and burned it to the ground. But the head librarian, Alexandria, and five of her most trusted aides escaped, saving as many books as possible. Your great-grandfather, Moonshadow

Riverwest, was one of those aides, and the books he rescued are our books.

One book was especially coveted by the enemy: one that supposedly could bring about the downfall of the Seelie Court or the Sluagh Horde. Alexandria knew that it was too important to destroy but too dangerous to fall into the wrong hands, and it and the most rare and valuable books she saved must be hidden until true scholars could keep them safe. Before she left, she gave each aide the location written in code and a codebook. When they or their descendants felt the time was right, they were to come together and bring the lost knowledge of the past back to the world. Such has been my mission, which I now pass on to you.

One more thing I need you to know: As much as I have loved books—and I have truly loved them—there's one thing I have loved more, and that is you, my darling little bookworm and dearest daughter.

—Dad

Shade gawped at the letter. *First I learn that my mother was one of the most feared warriors in all of Elfame, and now there's this! Do all parents keep secrets from their children?* she wondered.

"That explains the first sheet," Johannes beamed. "It is written in the book code!"

"The what?"

"The book code. The first number before the dash, this is the page in the book to turn to, and the second number, this is the vord on that page you use to make the message."

"Then let's do some translating," Shade said resolutely, trying to push her confused feelings about her father aside.

The two rifled quickly through the book, jotting down a word from the front and then one from the back and then one from the middle and then one from somewhere else, their fingers flying and their quill scribbling until the final word was written and they stopped and read: *squoosh up your face pick your nose then in the banana patch mambo dog faced.*

Shade frowned. "That doesn't make any sense."

Johannes cocked his head to the side in that way that kitties do when perplexed, like your cats, Mr. Wellington and Major Tom, did the day your mother brought your baby sister home from the hospital and held her in front of them. (As you recall, they weren't that impressed, but then she was a baby, and babies are inherently unimpressive except in their abilities to make an immense amount of noise and to expel a surprising number of vile-smelling substances.) "Ja. It is the gobbledygook."

Shade stared at the words, hoping that somehow they would change as she stared at them, just as the letter had sprung into view. This time, however, nothing changed. Then she thought of the letter. "There were five aides, right?"

"Ja."

"And each one was given a copy of this coded message and a book and were told that one day they would find one another and go find the hidden books."

"Ja."

"That's it! Radishbottom's book isn't the key to the code—it's *one* of the keys to the code. Each fairy must have been given a different book. Some of the numbers in the message come from this book and some must come from each of the other four. The only way to translate it is to have all five books and then figure out which words from which books make sense together."

"And how are ve to find out vhat the other four books are?"

Shade crossed her arms. "I'm going to do what my father wanted me to do. I'm going to find the other bookkeepers, whoever and wherever they are."

"And vhere vill you start looking?"

Shade's face dropped as she realized that she had no idea. She looked down, dejected, then she noticed a word hastily scrawled in pencil on the back of her father's note: "Cottinghamtownshireborough." She jabbed the word with her finger. "That's where."

Johannes looked at her, eyes wide with admiration.

Then he cocked his head. "And do you know vere Cottinghamtownshireborough is?"

"No. Fortunately, we've got a lot of books here that can tell me where it is." She turned on her heel and marched out of the room.

5

In which everybody's favorite ne'er-
do-wells return . . .

A quick peek at a couple of maps revealed that
Cottinghamtownshireborough was a small fairy
village in the northeast, not far from the door
marked "Meadowbrook." In spite of her resolute
words, Shade was hesitant to go. As much as she
wanted to fulfill this great dream that had been shared
by three generations in her family, she really didn't
want to leave the comforts and joys of the library.

Living and working there fulfilled her childhood dreams, and she had risked so many dangers to get there. The library had more books than could be read in a lifetime and intelligent people to talk about them with. What more could anyone want?

But this is what Dad would want, Shade concluded. *I have to do it for him.*

Shade rushed off to share the news with the head librarians only to discover Émilie gone and François locked in his office with Dewey, trying to organize a children's section as quickly as possible. "I think it best that ve tend to the library business and discuss things when ve close tonight, ja?" Johannes suggested. Shade agreed and tried to focus on her duties but instead spent most of her time looking at the clock, awaiting closing time. It's much like the time when you failed that math quiz and accidentally tied your shoe to your desk at school because you were too eager for the night to come so that you could see your sweet little Nana Svetlana's debut (and, as it turned out, final) performance as a trapeze artist.

But eventually the end of the workday came. After locking all the library doors in record time, Shade flew up to the head librarians' office where Johannes had gathered everyone. François and Dewey hunched over a library floor plan, Émilie watched the sun set over the vast western sea through the picture window, Johannes paced, and Caxton leaned back in a chair with his feet up on Émilie's desk as he tossed playing card after playing card into his bowler hat several feet away from him.

"Ze Great Library of Alexandria?" François gasped, as Johannes and Shade shared their discovery. He put his coffee cup down, much to everyone's surprise, and rushed over to an equally shocked Émilie and grabbed her hands. "Ze Great Library of Alexandria!"

"*Oui*," she said. A marble tear slid down her cheek then clattered on the floor. She turned to the others. "As children, we both heard tales of the great lost library run by the beautiful and wise Alexandria. It inspired us to create this place."

"And we 'ave read and 'eard ze rumors of books

saved from ze great burning, but now we discover zem to be true!"

"Looks like it," Shade said. "And I'm going to track them down."

"*Mais oui! Absolutement!*" François agreed. "We must track down ze books!"

"Great!" Shade replied. "Who's coming with me?"

Suddenly, the excitement drained from everyone's face.

"Em . . . well, I wish I could go," François said. "But I 'ave ze children's section to create, plus ze day-to-day operations of ze library and—"

"And 'e don't like bein' outside." Caxton chuckled.

"But he's a gargoyle," Shade said, suddenly realizing she had never actually seen François step outside. "Aren't gargoyles supposed to protect buildings and—"

"I protect *zis* building," François declared indignantly. "I just do it from ze inside. Just because I 'ave a touch of ze agoraphobia—"

"And he's afraid of heights," Dewey added.

"And why don't you go, zen?" François snapped at Dewey.

"I can't—this children's section is going to mean a *massive* reorganization." He rubbed his hands in anticipation.

Shade turned to the lady of stone. "Émilie?"

Émilie shook her head sadly. "Today I have spoken to representatives of the Seelie and the Sluagh and fear that Grand Scrutinizer Drabbury will be as big of a problem as he would have us believe. François and I simply cannot leave as long as he is a threat."

"Johannes? Caxton?" Shade asked.

"It is the spring, ja? I'm sorry, but I cannot be going," Johannes sighed. "I have the seasonal allergies."

"But you live in a tree," Shade pointed out.

"It is a library tree. That is different."

Shade frowned. "And you, Caxton?"

"Sorry, love. Can't go."

"And why not?"

"Oi don't wanna."

"Fine!" Shade huffed. "I'll just go on my own. I'll leave tomorrow."

"*Mais non, Mademoiselle Shade,*" Émilie said. "It could be dangerous. Let us wait for things to settle down, then we can find someone to accompany you."

"Nope. I'm going tomorrow and there's not a dingle-dangle thing you can do to stop me. I can take care of myself. Besides, I'm just going to a tiny town to find a secret bookworm. How dangerous could that be?"

As I'm sure you are aware, good Reader, declaring "How _____ could that be?" all but guarantees that whatever "that" is will, of course, end up being _____. In fact, the more confident the speaker is that "that" won't be _____, the _____er it tends to be, possibly even the _____est.

Suddenly, the sound of a door slamming made everyone jump. Then there was a loud scraping sound, as if someone were dragging something heavy over a wooden floor. The fairies hurried to the railing. Way down at the bottom of the library tree, a brownie in a too-tight brown suit and little hat and a thin pixie clad in a baggy green suit, overcoat, and top hat tossed chairs on top of two massive study tables that had been shoved against the door labeled "Jeroboam."

"Ginch? Professor?" Shade called down.

Both fairies stopped mid-chair-fling and looked up. "'Ey, little Sprootshade!" the brownie, Rigoletto Ginch, shouted back. He nudged the pixie with his elbow. "Look, Professor! It's-a the Sprootshade!"

The two bounded up the ramp and leaped into Shade's arms, sending all three tumbling into the office. "Get off me, you dingle-dangle doofuses!" Shade shoved herself free, smiling in spite of herself. "What are you two doing here?"

Ginch dusted himself off. "Why, me and the Professor, we were a-talking—well, I was a-talking and he was a-listening because he no talk—and so I say to the Professor, 'You know who we no see in the long time? The little Sprootshade! We gotta go see the little Sprootshade and see how she do.'"

The Professor's stomach gave a loud growl. He put his hand to his belly and then, spying a tray full of acorns on Émilie's desk, leaped across the room on his grasshopper-like legs and stuffed an acorn in each cheek, making him look like a chipmunk. He was about to stuff in a third when Émilie said, "Please do not eat those—they are the acorns from which we grow the library trees."

The Professor stopped, gave her a thumbs-up, and instead shoved the acorn into a pants pocket. He then opened his other pants pocket and spat the two acorns in his cheeks into it and then finished by picking up a letter opener from the desk and tucking it up his coat sleeve.

"You just came to visit me, eh?" Shade said. "So what was that business downstairs with the tables and chairs?"

"Oh, that?" Ginch waved a hand dismissively. "That was just the simple misunderstanding."

"So you got caught stealing and now somebody wants to kill you," Shade said.

"Pretty much." The Professor whistled and mimed dealing cards. "Oh, and we do a little of the card-sharping too."

"How did you get in?" Johannes asked. "I vatched Fraulein Shade lock the doors."

The Professor stuck his hands in his pockets and pulled out a massive ring of keys with one hand and an equally massive ring of lockpicks with the other. Ginch shrugged. "I no know. She must have forgotten to lock that one."

Shade sighed and shook her head. "I can't believe I'm saying this, but how would you two knuckleheads like to go with me to find some lost books?"

Ginch and the Professor looked at each other and raised their eyebrows. "Does it involve going any place that's-a no Jeroboam?" Ginch asked.

"Yes."

Ginch and the Professor nodded. "It's-a the deal!" Ginch declared. He and the Professor spat into their hands and offered to shake with Shade.

"Um, ew, no," Shade said, making a face. "I'm not shaking your spitty hands."

Ginch and the Professor shrugged. "Okay, fine, little Sissy White Gloves," Ginch said. "We clean them then shake." The two licked their palms then held out their hands again.

Shade stood impassive as the two grinned expectantly at her. "Fine," Shade groaned, shaking each hand and then wiping hers on her shirt. "Why do I have the feeling this is a profoundly bad idea?"

The Professor held up his index finger, plunged a hand in a coat pocket, then pulled out a book: *The Lessons of History* by The Reverend Zinn.

"Oh yeah," Shade said with a weary nod. "That's why."

6

In which a walk is taken, sights are seen, and a ferret is pulled from someone's trousers . . .

The next morning, Shade, clad in her brown and green leather traveling attire, strode out the door marked "Meadowbrook" with Ginch and the Professor in tow. The morning sun peeked out from between fluffy clouds like a cheerful toddler trying to hide amongst a flock of sheep. Dew glistened on the grass. As they walked, Shade excitedly told the two tales about working at the library. Ginch, for his part, gave an animated (and largely embellished and self-aggrandizing) account of everything that he and the Professor had done since helping Shade find her way to the Grand Library, which more or less consisted of the two cheating at cards or stealing things and then having to run away to avoid arrest, imprisonment, or having their arms ripped off and being beaten to death with them.

"Have either of you ever thought about getting an honest job again?" Shade asked after one of Ginch's more harrowing accounts of escape. "You know, one that wouldn't almost get you killed on a regular basis?"

The two made faces similar to the one you made after trying your Aunt Tatiana's candied Brussels sprouts in blue cheese sauce. "Oh, no!" Ginch declared resolutely. "We no can-a be tied down like that. The thrill of adventure, it run through our veins. The road, she's-a the part of us."

The Professor pounded his chest and then lifted his shirt to show an elaborate map drawn on his torso.

"'Ey, look! We're just two freckles and a mole away from where we go." Ginch poked the Professor's stomach. The Professor clutched his belly and silently laughed.

Shade closed her eyes and shook her head to rid herself of the sight of the Professor's pale belly. "Okay, sapheads, save the tickle fight for later. We've got plenty of walking ahead of us."

And walk they did, for miles along a winding dirt road through lush green meadows and past freshly plowed fields where fairies sowed seeds. Some would have passed for elves except for their big furry cow ears, and others were clearly dwarves but unlike any Shade had ever seen before—dark-skinned, clean-shaven, either bald or with short-cropped hair.

Eventually they passed a lake, its placid blue surface glittering like a giant sapphire. On its banks, a group of female fairies in peasant dresses—dwarves with long braided hair, wrinkled gnomes in blue conical hats, and more cow-eared fairies—sat around a large flat stone on which they pounded wet mounds of cloth in time to a chanted song in a language Shade didn't recognize. She found it mesmerizing.

The lake, however, eventually tore Shade's attention away from the waulking song. Or rather, what came out of the lake. A little way from the shore, small waves formed and lapped upon the banks. Then something slowly rose from the depths. Shade elbowed Ginch. "What's that?"

From the water emerged something round, about the size of a bowling ball, and covered in short, white, curly fur, with two round red circles on either side. Drawing nearer to the shore, it rose further until, at last, there it was: the head of a cow. Shade could see what looked like gills on its neck just beneath its jaw. The cow opened its mouth, gave what sounded like a cross between a moo and a frog's croak, and trudged up the bank, shaking water from its white hide.

Ginch nodded toward it. "That's-a the cow."

"Gee, thanks. Couldn't have figured that out on my own."

"'Ey, I no know whatta you know and whatta you don't."

While the two bickered, a whole herd of aquatic cattle rose from the lake, moo-croaking off to munch on prairie grasses in the fields beyond, followed by two tall fairies. They would have looked just like humans if humans had webbed fingers and toes, gills, and completely black eyeballs, which humans don't. Except for your Uncle Arthur, of course, but I think we can both agree that he's a bit atypical to say the least.

As Shade, Ginch, and the Professor strolled down the road, away from the herd of fairy cattle and past several small farms, Shade—while quite eager to begin the great task she had inherited from her father—couldn't help but enjoy the rustic charms of farm country. "You know, this really reminds me of scenes in Ingalls the Wilder's book, *The Tiny Hut on the Grasslands*. Isn't it something?"

"Yeah, I no like it either," Ginch said. "I mean, if we gots to skeedeedle, I no see the place to hide."

The Professor nodded and then pulled his coat around him and up over his head.

"That's-a no good. I can still see the hat."

The hat swiftly disappeared into the collar of the Professor's overcoat.

"That's-a better."

Shade sighed and walked faster. Ginch followed, pulling the Professor, still hiding inside his coat, along by the sleeve. Eventually they spied a sign that read "Cottinghamtownshireborough," beyond which lay a sleepy hamlet consisting of quaint little houses, a few storefronts, a blacksmith's forge, a cooper's workshop, and an inn whose sign depicted a clean-shaven dwarf, a cow-eared fairy, and a fairy with gills and webbed hands dancing arm-in-arm-in-arm underneath the words "The Three Jolly Herdsmen." Aside from some fairy ponies tied to hitching posts, the road was empty.

"Okay, so last night I read some books on spies and secret societies—Sir Ian of Flemyng, Benedict Trenton, Handler the Unfortunate, and some others," Shade told Ginch and the Professor. "Keep your eyes and ears peeled for anything out of the ordinary. The fairy we're looking for could be anyone, and if they're as secretive as members of secret societies are supposed to be, it could take days, maybe even weeks, to ferret them out."

The Professor reached into his pants and pulled out a wriggling brown ferret. He stroked its fur a few times, kissed it on the head, and set it on the ground.

"Go find-a the secret book guy, little Reeki-Teeki-Teevee!" Ginch called as the ferret raced down the road and out of town.

Shade slapped her forehead. "Not that kind of ferret. I mean, we have to search around, quietly and discreetly, and figure out who the fairy is. But where do we start?"

Ginch pointed decisively at the inn. "That's-a where we start."

Shade was impressed. "You know, you're right. Pubs and taverns are the exact sorts of places where secrets get whispered, people who know people who know people congregate, information can be bartered for . . . Nice work, Ginch."

Ginch tucked his fingers in his vest and looked pleased with himself. "I no mean to be smart—I just wanna the drink. But since I'm-a the smart on accident, I think that means I'm even smarter than if I do it on purpose."

"Whatever. Let's go." But just before Ginch and the Professor could march into the inn, Shade grabbed them by the backs of their jackets and pulled them back. "Remember—we need to be subtle. This person is living in secret."

The Professor held up his index finger. He pulled three eye patches out of his pocket and slipped the first on.

"Ha-ha! That's-a the good idea!" Ginch laughed as the Professor put one on him. "We go in the disguise."

"What the dingle-dangle are you doing?" Shade slapped the Professor's hand away as he tried to fix an eye patch on her. "I'm not wearing that stupid thing. Remember: We're supposed to be subtle."

"Don't you worry. We'll be so subtle everybody gonna look at us and say, ''Ey, look at those three! Those are the most subtle fairies we ever see!'"

The Professor nodded vigorously, put on the eye

patch that Shade had refused so that both his eyes were covered, turned, and slammed right into the side of the building.

Ginch took the Professor by the shoulders and guided him through the doorway. "C'mon! This way, partner."

"Yeah, subtlest fairies ever," Shade muttered as she followed them inside. "This won't end well."

7

In which things do not end well . . .

Now if this were a proper story involving hidden tomes and secret societies, at this point I would get to describe a dark, dingy bar filled with criminals, ne'er-do-wells, spies, counterspies, counter-counterspies, secret agents (which, I'll have you know, are actually quite different from spies), and mercenaries, at least one of whom would be charming in a gruff sort of manner and who would no doubt by the end of the tale see the error of their ways, reform, and join the good fight. What's more, there would be a good deal of whispered conversations, coded messages, secret signals, and all manner of thrilling skullduggery. At this point, however, I would hope that you would know better than to expect anything of the sort from this terribly improper tale.

The Three Jolly Herdsmen was a cheerful place with sunlight streaming in through its many windows. Its clean wooden tables and benches were mostly empty, save for a quartet of cow-eared fairies playing cards near a large stone fireplace and a gnome playing checkers with a pipe-smoking fairy who exhaled smoke from the gills in her neck. Behind the immaculate bar stood a tan, clean-shaven dwarf whistling merrily as he polished it.

"I no like-a the looks of this place," Ginch muttered. "You no can-a trust any pub this clean."

"Now remember, play it cool," Shade whispered. "*Be subtle.*"

The Professor saluted and then, still wearing patches over both eyes, promptly strode toward the bar, banged loudly into a table, then tripped and fell over a bench, knocking it over. Shade groaned as every eye in the place turned toward them.

"Arternoon to thee, friends!" the bartender called. "What kin I get thee?"

The Professor whistled and held up three fingers before springing to the bar, lifting up an eye patch so that he could see the way. "My partner says three meads," Ginch explained.

"No thanks," Shade said. "I don't want a drink."

"Who said any of those were for you?" Ginch asked as the Professor took the first mug the bartender filled and put it in a pants pocket, tucked the second in his jacket, and thirstily guzzled the third. "I'll take one myself, paisan."

As the bartender filled another mug and slid it to Ginch, the Professor pointed to a jar of pickled eggs.

"Help thyself," the bartender said. The Professor stuffed three into his mouth before loading his pockets with the rest. "What brings thee to Cottinghamtown-shireborough, friends?"

Having done her reading on spycraft and secret societies, Shade knew it was important to have a cover story, preferably one that made you seem as innocent and harmless as possible. Because of that, she was ready for the very question the bartender asked. What she was not prepared for, however, was for Ginch to give a little belch and say, "We're-a lookin' for somebody in the secret society of book guys. You know him?"

"Ginch!" Shade punched him hard in the arm. "What're you dingle-dangle doing?"

"'Ey! Whatta you do, fatcha-coota-matchca, sproot!" Ginch objected, rubbing his shoulder. "Do we look for the secret book society spy guy or do we no look for the secret book society spy guy?"

"Yes, we do, but we were supposed to be *subtle*!"

"I was-a the subtle!"

"You think that was subtle?" Shade put her hands on her hips and glared.

Ginch stared back at her. He blinked a couple of times and then cleared his throat. "Okay, maybe I'm-a no sure what 'subtle' means."

Shade groaned and thumped her head down on the bar.

"Thou're lookin' for a member of a secret society or summat?" the bartender asked.

"Yeah," she replied wearily.

"Thou'll be wantin' Poor Richard then."

Shade's head shot up. "Wait—you know you have a member of a secret society here and you know who he is?"

"Oh, aye. Every fairy in Cottinghamtownshireborough do. Ahoy the bar!" the bartender sang out. "Who do we know what's in a secret society, then?"

"Poor Richard," all the other fairies replied, not looking up from their games.

"How do all of you know this?" Shade asked, quite bewildered.

"Poor Richard. He tells everyone who'll listen he's part of a secret society. Truth be told, we all stopped payin' it any mind ages ago. He's a rum 'un, but a good bloke. Organized the local fire brigade, he did."

"And local school," called out one of the cow-eared fairies.

"And he lends out his books to anyone wants readin'," the gnome added.

"Aye, good bloke." The gilled fairy took a thoughtful puff from her pipe. "Rum 'un, but a good bloke."

"You couldn't . . . oh, I don't know . . . tell us what he looks like? Maybe where we could find him?" Shade asked, trying to play it cool. To be honest, she was a little disappointed—just as I am, and I'm sure you are—that it had been so easy to find her fairy, having expected something more exciting like in adventure stories she had read, and part of her hoped that the bartender would suddenly look nervous and maybe clam up or insist on speaking to her in private.

But she (and I and you, dear Reader) once again had her hopes dashed when the bartender loudly and plainly replied, "Oh, aye. He's a cowlug like that lot playin' cards. Old as the hills and right pudgy, he is, with long gray hair except on top where he's bald as a shaved egg."

"Don't forget that balmy hat o' his," one cowlug added.

"Right, probably wearin' that beaver-skin hat of his. Just head up road a spell and look for his signs," the bartender said.

"This time o' day, thou'll be wantin' that barn he mucks about in and not the house," the gnome suggested.

"Aye, the barn," the bartender agreed knowingly. "And don't mind any loud noises thou might hear—that's just Poor Richard blowing summat up. Perfectly safe . . . least that's what he says."

Shade found all that they said quite strange but it all made a good deal of sense a little while later when she, Ginch, and the Professor came across a pair of signs, one pointing north to a sagging, gray, two-story house that looked on the verge of collapse and the other pointing south to a dirt path that led through a small copse of trees. The north-pointing sign, an elegant one with carved letters and polished wood, read:

DOMUS DOCTRINA

HOME OF RICHARD FREEHOLDER

FAIRY OF LETTERS, INVENTOR,

FIREFIGHTER, LIBRARIAN, EDUCATOR,

PHILANTHROPIST,

& SECRET SOCIETY MEMBER

The other sign, a much less grandiose affair, was a simple, rough-hewn board on a pole reading: "Laboratory: Proceed with caution. Fireproof clothing encouraged but not required."

"The fairies at the bar said he'd be in a barn," Shade said. "Do you think that could be the lab?"

As if in answer to her question, something boomed loudly beyond the trees.

"Come on!" Shade headed down the path.

Ginch made no show to move. "I'll-a stay here and keep the watch. My clothes, they're-a no the fireproof and too nice to risk."

"Professor?"

The Professor scratched his head. He took out a match, lit it, and held it to one of his coat sleeves.

When the sleeve caught fire, he frantically waved it, blew on it, and finally swatted it out with his other hand. After that, he shrugged and headed off into the trees with Shade close behind.

After a minute's jog, Shade and the Professor found a grassy pasture in the middle of which stood a barn, its paint faded and peeling, its sides and roof covered in ivy and moss. In front of the barn was a scorched patch of grass with a tangle of melted wires and shards of broken glass at its center. A few feet away from the burnt grass lying spread-eagled with his face turned up to the bright afternoon sun was a bald, wrinkled old fairy, the long gray hair that grew from the sides and back of his head fanned out to either side underneath his black-and-white spotted cow ears. On his chest sat a ferret that, upon seeing the Professor, leapt into his arms. The Professor hugged the ferret, kissed his head, then stuffed him back into his pants.

"Oh my gosh!" Shade rushed over to the fairy. Wisps of smoke curled up from his simple brown homespun jacket and trousers. "Are you all right?"

The jowly face of the fairy grinned. "Oh, quite all right! Quite all right, indeed!" he chuckled.

"Do you need any help?"

The fairy squinted his blue eyes up at Shade and the Professor. "Need? No, don't believe I *need* help, but I will most gratefully accept it. If one of you would be kind enough to help me to my feet and the other find my glasses and hat, I would be much obliged."

Shade strained to help Poor Richard to his feet, then he stood and leaned heavily on a walking stick. The Professor plopped a round fur hat (now rather singed) on the cowlug's head, slid a pair of round wire-rimmed glasses onto his nose, and gave the chubby old fairy a thumbs-up. Poor Richard's eyes lit up and he grasped the Professor's hand.

"Why, it's Professor Pinky, the foremost authority on intra- and extra-spatial studies! I'm not sure if you remember, but we met once when I was presenting a paper on practical galvanism at the University of Streüseldorff many years ago. And who is it that you have with you?" Poor Richard turned to Shade. His eyes widened in pleasant surprise. "My goodness, it's been an awfully long time, but I have seen those eyes before. Tell me, child, are you Moonshadow's granddaughter or great-granddaughter?"

"Wait, you knew my great-grandfather?" Shade was stunned. "Then you're . . ."

"One of the librarians of the Great Library? I am indeed." As Shade gawped, Poor Richard winked at her. "Or were you going to say very, very old? If so, guilty as charged."

"But how—"

"How have I lived to be so old? There's no great trick to it, my dear—you just have to keep not dying and there you are. But I believe we may have more pressing concerns. If you are here, I assume that you are gathering together G.L.U.G., are you not?"

"Glug?"

"Yes, the Great Library's Unseen Guardians. I know, it's a terrible acronym but we were in a bit of a hurry at the time—as we may be now. You didn't happen to try to break into my house before coming to the lab, did you?"

"No! We would never do that," Shade replied. The Professor gave a whistle and pointed to his own chest. "Okay, he would, but he didn't."

"Yes, the Professor's personal peccadilloes are well-known in academic circles. Well, if it wasn't the two of you—"

"How do you know someone broke in?"

The cow-eared fairy pointed to a red flag attached to a hinge on the side of the barn. "One of my little inventions. The flag goes up if someone tries to break in through any of the doors or windows of my house, which it did a little while ago. I would have gone to investigate, but I was in the middle of my experiment and thought it could wait."

The Professor pointed to the scorched patch and melted and broken equipment and cocked an eyebrow.

"The experiment? I was capturing lightning in a jar."

Shade frowned. "Doesn't look like you did."

"My dear, failure is always a necessary pit stop on the road to success."

Shade pointed her thumb back toward the road. "Shouldn't we—"

Before she could finish her question, Ginch came charging through the trees. "'Ey, everybody! The house is on fire! And there's-a the Sluagh red cap goons a-standing around watching!"

"They must not have appreciated my various anti-theft devices. Oh well, come with me," Poor Richard said, hobbling over to the barn and sliding its doors open to reveal a sizable cart filled with books and scientific instruments and a pair of ponies in stalls. "If you'll help me with my ponies, we'll ride posthaste to safety."

While Shade and the Professor hitched up the fairy ponies, Poor Richard climbed up onto the driver's seat of the cart and fiddled with a variety of knobs and levers, and Ginch poked through the various odds and ends in the back. "'Ey, why you got alla the junk in the trunk here? You always stay ready to make-a the break for it?"

"Only for the past month or so," the old fairy answered. "When Whippitie's grandson came by and said that he was finding all of us G.L.U.G.ers and getting ready to go after the hidden books, I thought I should prepare—"

"Hold on," Shade said. "Another member of the secret society found you?"

"Oh, yes, but then I haven't made myself terribly hard to find, have I? But I'm not sure that now is the time to get into all of that, for there is a time for discussion and a time for action, and the wise know the difference. I don't claim to be terribly wise, but I believe having Sluagh hooligans burning down one's house would be a call to action, especially since the fire will eventually reach my chemical and gunpowder stockpile."

An explosion ripped through the springtime quiet.

"The fire has apparently reached my chemical and gunpowder stockpile," Poor Richard said matter-of-factly. "Right, everybody in."

Ginch and Shade scrambled up to sit beside Poor Richard on the driver's bench, and the Professor hopped into the back and settled in amongst the junk. With a flick of the reins, they rattled off through the meadow and the trees and back to the main road, from which they could see green flames rapidly consuming Domus Doctrina while goblins in red caps, a lean, blue-haired elf in bronze armor, and an immense, hairy ogre stood gathered around it. They could also see, much to their horror, the armored fairy turn their way and point as if to say, "Get them!"

8

In which there is a wagon ride
much more exciting than the one
you took on that school visit to the
apple orchard . . .

"I'm-a something of the expert on skeedeedling,"
Ginch informed Poor Richard as he looked with
dismay toward the fairy gang. "And right now,
we really gotta skeedeedle!"

"I'm much of your opinion, my good fellow," Poor

Richard agreed. "One of the most important keys to success in life is knowing when to leave."

"We're not going to have a dingle-dangle life to succeed in if we don't leave a little faster!" Shade pointed behind them. "That ogre is almost on us!"

Now good Reader, I know that you are quite the expert on fairies and fairy lore and know that ogres are fierce creatures covered in coats of short coarse hair except for the long, shaggy manes that flow down from their immense heads and the long, bushy beards that hang from their chins, that they usually stand around seven feet tall, and that they eat nothing but meat—preferably fresh fairy or human meat—so I won't bother going through all that. I will note, however, that this was a particularly large, vicious, and filthy ogre, its blood-red fur green in places from the algae growing in it and its rotten brown teeth on full display as it roared, charging down the hill and onto the road after them.

"An ogre, eh?" Poor Richard flicked the reins to spur the ponies to go faster but otherwise seemed unconcerned that a gigantic enraged cannibal was hot on their heels. He considered the levers and buttons in front of him. "I believe some tribuli should do the trick."

He pulled down a lever and a panel on the back of the cart opened, spilling little metal jacks, much like the ones your brother often plays with and fails to pick up. Unlike those jacks, however, these were sharpened into wicked points. The ogre stepped square onto them with one of its bare feet. It grabbed its foot, hopped around on the other, howled in pain, then, in a bizarre attempt to ease the pain, stuffed its injured foot in its mouth to suck on it. How effective such treatment could be, however, we will sadly never know for as it did so, its other foot landed on another jack, causing the ogre to fall onto its back and almost choke to death on its own foot.

"Do all of those levers and buttons do stuff like that?" Shade asked.

"Oh, I should say they do," Poor Richard laughed. "This is an all-purpose, ready-for-anything escape cart."

"Why would you build something like this?"

"Why, to escape, of course! Ever since Whippitie's grandson got in touch with me, I knew that trouble might—"

A whistle from the Professor interrupted him. Far behind, goblins and the armored fairy galloped after them.

"I think we gotta the bigger problems than who's a-talkin' to who," Ginch said, as the cart clattered onto the streets of Cottinghamtownshireborough.

"No worries, my good fellow. Just push that button in front of you."

Ginch did so and oil sprayed out of nozzles on the bottom of the cart, covering the cobblestone street behind them. When the first goblin war ponies hit the oil, they began to slip and slide until they fell on their sides and dumped their goblin riders painfully to the ground.

"Careful out here! It's slippery!" Poor Richard shouted as they passed the Three Jolly Herdsmen. "Soap and water should fix things right up!"

As the cobblestone street gave way once more to dirt road, Shade thought they were in the clear, but then more goblins and the armored fairy came galloping onto the road behind them. "What do we have to do to get away from these stupid termite-lickers?"

Poor Richard chuckled. "Sounds like someone inherited Moonshadow's temper. Might I suggest pulling that lever here?"

Shade pulled and clouds of gray, foul-smelling smoke billowed out of pipes on both sides of the cart. Their pursuers disappeared from view, although they could be heard coughing and gagging. The smoke continued to spew out until Poor Richard pushed the lever up. "That should do the trick."

It did not, however, for the armored elf emerged from the smoke cloud behind them, a long spear in her hand. "'Ey, cowboy, you got any other tricks in this jaloopy!" Ginch cried.

"Tenacious one, isn't she?" Poor Richard said. "Well, I think it's time I show her what happens when you attack an inventor!"

Poor Richard pushed a button just as the armored fairy flung her spear. A panel running on the back of the cart unhooked and was about to swing down when the spear pinned it in place.

"Hey, Richard, what did that button do?" Shade asked.

"It began the ignition sequence for the assault fireworks I have set to launch from the back of the cart."

"And what happens if the panel in the back doesn't open?"

"Oh, my dear, that would never happen. I have it spring-loaded to open and—"

"Just answer the question!"

"Well, I suppose the whole cart would explode."

"Puckernuts!"

"Why do you ask?"

"Because that's exactly what's about to happen!" Shade's mind raced, trying desperately to come up with a way to survive both Poor Richard's mad inventions and the even madder villain pursuing them. "Ginch, Professor—get yourselves and Richard on those ponies and cut loose the cart!"

"'Ey, wait a minote!" Ginch objected. "What about you? We gotta—"

"Just do what I say!" Shade said, grabbing a long bronze rod from the equipment piled in the cart. "I'll be fine!"

Ginch nodded. "'Ey, Professor! Give us the hand here!"

The Professor pulled a wooden hand out of his coat pocket and tossed it to Ginch, who slapped it away. "We no gotta the time for the jokes, partner! C'mon!"

The Professor climbed over the clutter, grabbed Poor Richard around his squishy belly, and sprang onto one of the ponies. Ginch leaped onto the other one. The Professor pulled out a long cavalry sword and sliced through the traces connecting the ponies to the cart, pulled out a bugle, and blew a call to charge on it as the ponies galloped furiously away from the cart.

Meanwhile, Shade opened her wings, soared high, then looped around and down, coming up fast behind the armored fairy. She swung the bronze rod with all her might at the fairy's head. Had Shade been a more active and sporty fairy, like the majority of the residents of Pleasant Hollow, she no doubt would have struck their pursuer a devastating blow, thus ending the chase and saving the day. But Shade wasn't—she would always rather curl up with a book than go outside and toss around an acorn, play grubstick, and such—so it should come as no surprise that she didn't even come close to hitting the fairy. All she succeeded in was accidentally and painfully banging her toes on the rider's bronze-clad shoulder as she glided past.

In a flash, the rider drew her sword. "Come back here and fight, Little Owlet!" the fairy shouted. That phrase, "Little Owlet," sent a shock through Shade, but just then she didn't have the time to worry about it.

"Get donkled, snotbucket!" Shade called back as the rider came up fast on the back of the cart, which was slowing more and more now that it had been cut loose from its ponies. "And you might want to look where you're going!"

Shade's fairy foe turned just in time for her pony to slam into the back of the cart and send her sailing over the pony's head. The pony shook itself and ran off into the grass as sparks shot out the edges of the cart's speared back panel. As Shade flew away from the cart, it exploded in a massive blooming of multicolored sparks and flames. The armored fairy shot through the air in a long arc, landing a hundred yards away with a loud crash and clatter.

By the time Shade caught up with the others, they had left the road and were well on their way back to the Grand Library. "'Ey, little Sprootshade! You make it! We never had-a the doubt!" Ginch cried.

The Professor whistled and pointed to the palm of his hand. Ginch frowned and tossed him a gold coin. "Okay, maybe I have-a the one doubt, but I'm-a still glad to see you. We hear the big, big boom and we worry a little."

"Yes, minor design flaw that," Poor Richard muttered, stroking his chin. "Should be easy enough to—"

"That can wait," Shade said. "We need to go back now and find your codebook, Richard. The protection spell on it is strong enough to survive that fire, right?"

"No need to go back. I always say that a good book should be kept close to your heart. In the case of my codebook . . . " Richard reached inside his jacket and pulled out a book: *Uncommon Nonsense* by Thomas Ache. " . . . I mean that in a very literal sense, and I encourage you to do the same with yours. Now let us make our way to a safe and quiet place as soon as possible, for we have much to discuss."

9

In which a bugbear once again
bugs people . . .

The Grand Library was, it seemed, a very safe place. However, when the four fairies entered, it was not as quiet as anyone would have liked.

"Again, I demand that you turn over every book on this list." Grand Scrutinizer Norwell Drabbury jabbed a stack of parchment on top of Johannes's circulation desk so hard that his talon pierced all the sheets and dug into the wood. "If you do, I will take it as an act of good faith and I can give you more time to enact the other required reforms."

"Again, we must refuse," Émilie said, her voice as smooth and unyielding as the marble from which she was made. "You may check out whatever you wish, as anyone may—"

"Which is one problem we must fix," Drabbury huffed.

"But we will not allow the permanent removal of a single text," Émilie finished, her voice now flintier than before she had been interrupted.

"Oh my goodness! A bugbear! I don't believe I've ever laid eyes on one. Fascinating." Poor Richard hobbled over and tapped one of Drabbury's elbow spikes with his walking stick. Drabbury yanked back his arm and growled. His eyes glowed red behind his dark glasses. Richard went on. "Cunning, powerful, aggressive, wickedly sharp talons and teeth, arm stingers filled with one of the deadliest venoms in all Elfame . . . curable only by unicorn horn, I believe."

"All true." Drabbury's lip curled in a proud, sneering smile.

"Yet the species is known for its immense insecurity, vanity, arrogance, and overwhelming need to prove its own—"

"And who, pray tell, are you?"

Poor Richard smiled as if engaged in the most pleasant of conversations. "Richard Freeholder of Cottinghamtownshireborough, although most refer to me as 'Poor Richard' because—"

"Ah. 'Poor' Richard Freeholder. You've been mentioned in a number of M.O.A.N. reports."

"Well, it's always nice to be remembered."

"Not in our reports it's not. In fact—" Drabbury stopped as a rat-faced goblin in a traveler's cloak who had just come through the Pleasant Hollow door waved him over. "Excuse me."

"There's no excuse for you, bugbutt," Shade fired after Drabbury.

He bared his teeth but said nothing as he went to join the rat-faced goblin, who whispered something in his ear. Drabbury pointed to the door, and the goblin left. Drabbury followed but first he declared loud enough for all to hear, "I have business to attend to. This library is not the only threat that M.O.A.N. must deal with, but make no mistake—it is a threat. And threats *will be dealt with*."

"Yeah, well, he who smelt it, he's-a the one who dealt it!" Ginch called after him. The Professor pinched his nose and waved his hand toward Drabbury as if trying to air out an unpleasant odor.

Drabbury slammed the door to Pleasant Hollow behind him.

Ginch shook his head. "That's-a one angry bug-a-the-boo."

"You have no idea, Monsieur Ginch," Émilie sighed before gliding off.

The Professor took a yellow stuffed bear wearing a little red shirt out of his coat and hugged it. Ginch patted him on the back. "Yeah, I like-a that one much better too."

Shade put her hands on her hips. "Okay, now's not the time for a teddy bear snuggle party—"

The Professor's eyes lit up. He clapped and started pulling bear after bear out of his pockets.

Ginch slapped his shoulder. "She say not now, partner."

The Professor pouted and made puppy-dog eyes at Shade.

"Fine! You go do whatever." The Professor gathered up all the bears and dashed off with Ginch shuffling a deck of cards behind him. Shade turned to Poor Richard. "Come on. You and I need to talk."

•

"With the Great Library under siege, Alexandria gathered up the most important books and fled," Poor Richard explained over a mug of hot chocolate in one of the library's reading lounges. "Before she left, she gave each of us—myself, your great-grandfather Moonshadow, Whippitie Stourie, Grigor Byrrower, and Máire Bowser—a copy of her intended hiding place for those books and our codebooks, then told us to scatter without telling the others where we were going or what book we were given. We were to remain hidden until the time was right for us all to find one another."

Shade frowned. "And so your idea of remaining hidden was to put up a sign that says 'Secret Society Member' and to tell everyone who will listen that you're a member of a secret society?"

The old fairy took a sip of his chocolate. "Mmm-hmm. Hiding in plain sight. The others—or their descendants—could easily find me, but who else would expect an actual secret society member to announce that he's the member of a secret society? Sometimes being bold and obvious is the sneakiest thing one can do."

"Or the dumbest." Shade shook her head in disbelief.

"My dear, for over four hundred seasons, I went undetected by both friend and foe."

"And then your house was burned to the ground and you had to run for your life."

Poor Richard nodded thoughtfully. "Yes . . . well, I suppose even cleverness has its limits."

"Now before everything went to slug snot, you said

somebody wanted to gather everyone together?" Shade asked.

"Yes. Martinko, the grandson of our head research librarian, Whippitie Stourie, visited me just a few weeks ago. He believed that now was the time for us to gather and track down Alexandria's books. I believe it was this place that inspired him." Poor Richard paused to gaze about the room. His eyes teared up. "So wonderful . . . I do believe it exceeds even what we built so long ago."

"So this Martinko might know where to find everyone else?"

"Oh, I have little doubt about that. First, he's a mummart, and like his grandmother and many of his fairy species, excellent at uncovering secrets. Second, his grandmother was probably the most gifted researcher Elfame's ever seen, and I assume Martinko has tracked down most if not all of us. Even if he hasn't, I've always suspected that Whippitie had a master list of all the codebooks. Find Martinko, and I believe we find the location of the lost books."

"And how are we supposed to find Martinko?"

"Oh, that's easy enough—we go to Gypsum-upon-Swathmud," Poor Richard replied offhandedly. "That's where he was off to."

"Gypsum?" Shade asked, a little surprised. "That's near where I grew up."

"No doubt he was chasing down a lead on you. And by my reckoning, he should have arrived in Gypsum days ago."

Shade slapped the end table next to her. "Right then. Let's go!"

Poor Richard gulped his mouthful of chocolate. "Excuse me?"

"I said, 'Let's go!' We're going to Gypsum immediately."

"Oh, I don't think so," Poor Richard said.

"What?" Shade frowned and crossed her arms. "Why not?"

"I'm a very old fairy and my achy bones had quite a jounce during our little adventure. We could all use a good dinner, a good night's sleep, and a good breakfast before we depart, for an empty belly often leads to an empty head, and a wearied mind tends to be a wandering one."

"Come on! These books have been hidden for generations!"

"And so waiting until morning is little more than a teardrop added to the great western sea," Poor Richard said. "As a free fairy, you may, of course, do as you please. I, however, shall not stir from this wondrous place until tomorrow."

Shade scowled at him, but the cowlug merely smiled contentedly, sipping his chocolate. "Fine! We leave right after breakfast, but it's dingle-dangle stupid to wait when we could go *now*."

"A most sensible decision, my dear Shade. And no need to work yourself up. What harm could one night's delay really do?"

10

In which we find out what harm
one night's delay could really do . . .

The next morning, already grumpy at having to wait
until morning, Shade became even grumpier when
she learned Poor Richard preferred to sleep in ("If
the sun does not yet shine, stay in that bed of thine," he
mumbled when she tried to rouse him early), and she
had reached her limit as Poor Richard's preferences for
generous portions and second, third, and fourth help-

ings made breakfast last well past when the library opened. "Would you hurry it up, cow-slug," Shade grumbled. "You too, brownie-butt and pixie-pants."

Ginch gave an appreciative belch and patted his belly. "I'm-a done. Professor?"

The Professor stuffed a sausage in his mouth, tucked hard-boiled eggs, toast, and a pot of jam in various pockets, then emptied a platter of bacon into his top hat before putting the hat back on and saluting.

Poor Richard sighed contentedly. "Just one more of these delightful—"

Suddenly they heard a scream from the main floor. Shade dashed out of the dining hall and sailed over the railing to see what the matter was. A small thin fairy—a mummart with a shock of white hair and long spindly arms and legs, his clothes tattered and muddy—was collapsed on the ground. The black-cloaked elfin boy knelt next to him while the green-cloaked elfin girl, with a confidence that belied her young years, commanded, "Keep back! Everyone give them space!"

Shade alighted next to the fallen fairy. "What happened?"

The fairy's eyes grew wide. "You . . . The one I was . . . " he whispered weakly. The mummart pulled a leather-bound book and a small, tattered notebook from his coat and held them out to Shade, blood beading along a wicked scratch on the back of his hand. "They have the list and the code sheet. . . but not my . . . and they know about . . . Bowser twins in Bilgewater . . . Grigor's tomb . . . but not you . . . "

The mummart shook, foam frothing from his mouth. "He's been poisoned!" the elf boy shouted. "We need a wizard who can cast a stasis spell and a healer! Now!"

A small owl-headed goblin in robes holding a staff rushed over, chanting and making intricate gestures with his staff, which glowed with orange light. The chant completed, the wizard touched the staff to the mummart's chest. The light spread over the fairy's body. Immediately, his convulsions ceased.

The wizard wiped his brow. "The poison, whatever

it is, is especially nasty. I was able to slow its spread, not stop it completely."

"How long do we have?" Shade asked.

"If you're lucky, a week. Probably more like days. You need to get him an antidote as quickly as possible."

"I know an excellent physician," the elf girl in green declared.

"As do I," said the elf boy in black. The two looked at each other with curiosity and then ran, one to the door marked "Ande-Dubnos," the other to the one labeled "Dinas Ffaraon."

Shade heard the tapping of a cane behind her. "I heard cries for a healer, and while I'm not necessarily one, my studies have been quite wide and I do—" Poor Richard stopped talking abruptly upon seeing the unconscious fairy. "Martinko!"

"He's been poisoned," Shade explained.

"Then let's get our poor brother-in-arms someplace out of the way where I can examine him."

•

Shade waited for Poor Richard and the doctors fetched by the young elves—one wore the green livery and white rose of the Seelie Court, the other the black livery and red rose of the Sluagh Horde—to come out with news of Martinko's condition. The library was especially busy, as it had been for the past several days, so her duties managed to occasionally distract her, but she mostly brooded over the unexpected dangers of finding Alexandria's hidden books. *Martinko could die. I could die. All of my friends could die. What have I gotten us into? And who's out to get us?*

Then a memory sprang into her mind. "Little Owlet," the leader of the Sluagh gang had called her in Cottinghamtownshireborough. Shade frowned as she thought of Lady Perchta, the scarred Sluagh noblewoman who had vowed to get revenge on her. *That's what* she *called me. Is it just a coincidence, or . . . could Perchta be the one hunting down the book guardians?*

Shade shuddered, then turned her attention to Martinko's two books. The first, bound in green leather, bore the title *Jacob & Wilhelm's Grim Tales*. Shade used the book to decode Alexandria's message: "woe be unto those who dare tempt fate winning only ruined lives and dead souls."

"Just because 'grim' is in the title of the book . . . " Shade muttered as she then picked up the notebook Martinko had given her. Many of the pages had been torn out, leaving only blank ones behind. Studying those pages closely, she noticed a slight indentation on one. Remembering a trick Inspector Dupin used in *A Composition in Crimson*, Shade took a charred bit of wood from her fireplace and carefully rubbed it across the page. Soon the indentations became words in white surrounded by gray ash rubbings. It was a list of eight books: *Withering Depths*, *The Adventures of Hagan Finnegan*, *Jacob & Wilhelm's Grim Tales*, *Uncommon Nonsense*, *The Silver Sextant*, *The Adventures of the Dead Dead Gang*, *The Gallopville Yarns*, and *The Fairy Godfather*.

By the time she was finished, her smile of excitement was replaced by a frown of puzzlement, much like the look on your face when you unwrapped that present from your Aunt Esther you were sure would be that much longed-for shrunken head only to find it was a polished coconut shell, halved so that it could be used to make galloping sounds when playing at Holy Grail quests. Shade was about to say something so horribly rude that I would have refused to narrate it when, fortunately for us, a knock at her door made her turn. There stood Ginch, the Professor, and an exhausted Poor Richard.

"I'm afraid that the doctors—both admirable medical men and, interestingly, official physicians to the two royal courts—and I are quite baffled. Until we identify the exact poison used, which appears to be an exceedingly rare one, we can do nothing." The cowlug wiped a tear from his eye. "To see my good friend's grandson in such a state . . ."

Nobody said anything for a time until Shade awkwardly broke the silence. "So . . . Martinko gave me his codebook and this notebook, where I found this." She handed the page to Poor Richard. "At first I thought it was a list of all the codebooks but it can't be. There are too many here, plus mine's not even on the list."

Poor Richard picked up the notebook and fingered the stubs of the torn-out pages. "Oh, Whippitie, he's done you proud," he murmured. "I believe our Martinko has attempted to baffle our enemies by mingling the true books with a bunch of false ones. I wouldn't be surprised if he had a list of fifty or a hundred books that they'll have to sift through in their blind attempts to decode the message."

Ginch shook his head. "That would take-a the long, long time."

"But it's possible," Shade insisted. "With enough time, they *could* get hold of all those books and decipher it."

"Perhaps, although I believe Alexandria might have been even cagier than clever, clever Whippitie." Poor Richard took his copy of *Uncommon Nonsense* from his jacket where it had laid against his heart. "Would someone be so kind as to fetch a library copy of this?"

With a whistle and a salute, the Professor bounded

off on his spry grasshopper legs and returned just a minute later with the book.

"Thank you, my dear Professor. Now let us see something. Good Signore Ginch, would you please turn to page 48 and read the tenth word on the page."

Ginch flipped through the book, counted, and stabbed his finger on the page. "'And.'"

"Good. My dear Shade, please do the same with my copy."

Shade arched an eyebrow at him and then did as he asked. "'Equality.' Wait—"

The old fairy held up a hand. "Let us try another. Both of you: page 201 . . . let's make it words thirty and thirty-one."

"'Sunshine patriot,'" Shade read.

"'Try-ankle moon-archie,'" read Ginch.

Shade looked at Ginch's page. "That's '*tyrannical monarchy.*'"

"That's-a what I say: 'Try-ankle moon-archie.'"

"No, it's—never mind. What's going on, Poor Richard? Why don't the words match up?"

"Erratum. Alexandria must have given us all rare erratum copies—copies with misprints in them that throw off the word alignment. Ha-ha! The cleverness of that fairy. The cleverness of all my old friends. How I do miss them." Poor Richard looked down at the ground, his eyes glistening. He sniffed, wiped his eyes, and looked back up at Shade, Ginch, and the Professor. "So you see, even if Martinko included all five of the books on his list, it won't do our enemies any good— they must have our exact five codebooks to decode the message and find Alexandria's hiding place."

Shade smiled. All they had to do was track down two more books, both of which she knew the general locations of, while their foes spun themselves in circles looking through books that would only leave them more confused and further off course. Getting the lost books and fulfilling her father's lifelong goal seemed too easy.

However, as you no doubt know being such a wise and clever Reader, things that seem too easy—like decoupage, taxidermy, and sonnet writing—often turn out to be surprisingly difficult and bothersome. What's more, if solving the mystery of the lost books were too easy, this book would be done in a mercifully short time and we could all leave this unpleasantness behind and get on with our lives. But the writer of this dreadful story is far too cruel to let us off that easily, so I fear we must steel ourselves for setbacks, complications, and more improper adventures.

11

In which we learn the truth about
vacant lots, abandoned buildings,
and stores that seem smaller on the
inside than they should be . . .

"Right!" Shade said brightly, slapping her
hands together. "We have an advantage over
the thistlepricks we're up against. The book
list they've got is going to make them chase their own
tails for a while, so we should move before they get
wise. When they do smarten up, they'll probably go to

Bilgewater first, so we should go there right away and beat them to the punch. If we get going now—"

The Professor gave a two-note whistle and shook his head. "I agree with my partner," Ginch said. "It's almost nighttime and we no wanna be in the Bilgewater after dark."

Shade frowned and crossed her arms. "And why not?"

"Well, it's-a filled with the most sneaky, cheaty, crooked, no-good fairies in alla Elfame."

Shade smirked. "Well, then, it's a good thing I've got the two most sneaky, cheaty, crooked fairies in all of Elfame on my side."

The Professor blushed, batted his eyes, and waved a hand at Shade as if to say, "Oh, go on!"

Ginch, however, was not so easily flattered. "Maybe. But you also gotta the human beans runnin' around. You really wanna meet the human bean in the dark alley in the night?"

Shade blanched at this. She, like most fairies, was more than a little scared of human beings, which may sound silly to you, good Reader, especially if you're thinking specifically of your dear, sweet Aunt Agnes and her wonderful hand-knit socks—*So cute, so cozy!*—but fairies have good reason to fear us, as we are taller and stronger than almost every type of fairy and, more importantly and horribly for them, we can handle iron, the touch of which burns fairies as if it were red hot. Fortunately for them, we humans cannot see fairies except at certain times (dawn, dusk, Halloween, the Feast of St. Figgymigg, etc.) or under special circumstances (charming, abduction, being the half-nephew of a cheesemaker, and so forth). Because of this, most fairies prefer to live far away from humans or, if they do live amongst us, tend to stick to isolated farmhouses or tiny country villages in those rare places where the fairylands and our world overlap.

There are, however, some especially bold and cunning fairies who live largely unbeknownst to us in towns and even bustling cities. You know that vacant lot three blocks from your house? Or that corner of the public park where nobody ever plays? And those shops downtown that seem much smaller on the inside than they do on the outside, as if there were more space that you can't see? Well, more likely than not, all those places where nobody goes and that seem empty are, in fact, fairy buildings teeming with the most daring and thieving fairies around, for the main reason these fairies choose to live amongst us is to steal from us. Ever wonder why you always lose one of a pair of socks? Fairies steal them to use as sleeping bags and tea cozies. That half-sandwich you were saving that you think your brother Norbert ate? Possibly eaten by a fairy. *Possibly*, but in all likelihood it was Norbert, no matter what he claims—now that he's a teenager, he really does have the appetite of a starving hippopotamus with a tapeworm, doesn't he?

"No," Shade answered Ginch, "I do not want to run into a human in a dark alley at night. I also don't want another G.L.U.G.er to get attacked because we decided to get a good night's sleep and eat an extra-large breakfast. Is that what you want?"

Ginch shrugged. "I no know. Whatta we have for

the breakfast?" The Professor pulled out a menu and started pointing. "The Professor says he'll have-a the scrumbled eggs and the bacon, extra crispy, and—"

Shade slapped the menu out of the pixie's hands and glared at the two. "Well, I'm going right now. Alone, if I have to."

The Professor shoved his hands in his coat pockets and pouted. Ginch threw his hands up in the air. "Fine! Fine! We come with you. Fatcha-coota-matchca, sproot!"

"Unfortunately, I believe I must remain here," Poor Richard said with a sigh. "I fear my age would make me more of a hindrance than a help if action were in the offing. Besides, I must stay here and attempt to find a cure for poor Martinko."

So they headed out, stopping only to let Johannes know they were off in search of another book guardian. Just as she was about to walk away, Shade turned back, took Martinko's book list out of her pocket, and put it on the circulation desk. "Could you do me a favor? Could you and Caxton see who has checked out or even looked at these books in the past couple days and keep an eye on anyone new who takes an interest in them?"

Johannes read over the list. "This feels like skullduggery. And you know I am the great fan of skullduggery, mein friend. Ve vould be happy to do this! Vell, *I* vould be happy. Caxton—"

"Will bellyache about it, but he'll do it. Make sure the place doesn't burn to the ground while we're gone." And with that Shade and her friends strode through the door to Bilgewater.

•

They stepped out of the library tree on the edge of the seaside town, which was covered in a cold mist under a cloudy gray sky. Shade pulled her traveler's coat closer to ward off the cold. Bilgewater loomed ahead. Shade gulped. Six months ago, she felt overwhelmed when she first went to the goblin market of Gypsum-upon-Swathmud, but this place was even more intimidating with its colossal, human-sized buildings and, no doubt, its gigantic human inhabitants. *It'll be okay*, Shade reassured herself. *Hardly any humans can see us.*

"Ee, more o' yez?" asked a human who suddenly appeared out of the mist behind them carrying a canvas bag and a rifle. Shade, Ginch, and the Professor all jumped. "Bloody fairies."

"'Ey, whatta you do? You're-a no supposed to see us," Ginch said.

"Can't help it, la. Made the mistake o' loafin' and lookin' too mooch at a leaf o' grass on St. Whitman's day. Now mind—I've got me traps set doon by the stream and I'm right tired of yez lot turnin' oop in 'em."

"Maybe don't set traps near where fairies live," Shade said, eyeing his rifle warily.

"Maybe clear oot o' Bilgewater," the hunter grumbled in his thick accent, walking off. "Worse than bloody rats."

"'Ey, you know where we find somebody inna the secret society?" Ginch called after him. Shade swatted him on the arm. "Whatta you do? It worked in Cottinghamborough . . . shiretown . . . Whatever it's-a called, it worked there."

"Maybe," Shade conceded, "but that was a stupid little country town like the one I grew up in.

Bilgewater's a real, proper town—*and* one with humans. Any fairies running around here have got to be stealthy and cunning, which is what we've got to be as well. Got it?"

"Oh, we get it," Ginch assured her. The Professor nodded emphatically, pulled his black eye patches out of his pocket, and covered up one of his eyes and one of Ginch's. "See?" Ginch said. "We gotta the disguises, so we're ready to go a-sneakin' and a-snoopin'.'"

Shade slapped away the Professor's hands as he tried to fit an eye patch on her. When he tried to use it to cover up his other eye, Shade grabbed it. "Oh, no— we're not doing that again. Now let's go into town and see if we can find twins named Bowser."

Ginch and the Professor's eyes widened. They looked at each other and then at Shade. "Wait a minote! Bowser?"

"Yeah?"

"Regina and Ronnette Bowser?"

"Martinko didn't say any first names—he just said 'Bowser twins.'"

"So you tell us you look for the Bowser twins?"

"Yeah."

Ginch and the Professor frowned, crossed their arms, and shook their heads. "We're-a no lookin' for the Bowser twins."

Shade frowned and crossed her arms. "The donkle we aren't!"

"The donkle we is!" Ginch fired back. "The Bowsers are-a the crooks!"

"You're a couple of crooks!"

The Professor pointed to himself and Ginch and then held up his hand, his thumb and index finger about an inch apart. "Yeah, but we're-a the teensy-and-the-weensy crooks," Ginch explained. The Professor then stretched out his arms as wide as they could go. "Ginnie and Ronnie Bowser, they're-a the big, big crooks! Gangsters! They run the criminal umpire."

"Says who?"

"Says everybody. Now let's go back to the library and—"

"No. I'm going to find the Bowser twins."

"But it's-a no safe! They—"

"If they're keeping books safe, they can't be that bad. Look, I've got to do this and I'm going to do this with or without you," Shade said. And she meant it. Protecting those books and eventually bringing them back out into the world had been her father's lifelong goal, and Shade was going to do it or . . . *Well*, Shade thought, *I'm just going to do it. Best not to think of any other alternatives.* And so she marched into town.

It didn't take more than a minute for Shade to question the wisdom of that decision when a cart pulled by a huge draft horse almost ran her over. She leapt out of the way and was nearly trampled by a pack of filthy teenage boys in ragged clothing (they were very similar to your brother Norbert and his friends, except these boys were a bit grimier and actually spoke to one another and ran instead of shambling about zombie-like twiddling their little cellular telephones). Chasing them was a red-faced shopkeeper yelling about theft and making rude and questionable comments about the nature of their parentage.

Shade dashed out of the cobblestone street and flattened herself against the side of a building. From there, she watched the immense humans (well, immense to her, since she was about the size of your cat Major Tom if he were to stand on his hind legs, as opposed to your other cat, Mr. Wellington, who is still a kitten, although I do think he's catching up to Major Tom these days) bustling to and fro, hauling baskets of fish and clothes, peddling flowers and fruits, staggering from jobs or pubs, and just generally running about being terribly loud, big, and terrifying. She took a few deep breaths to calm her nerves. As her pulse slowed, she realized that none of the humans tromping past actually seemed to notice that she was there. Granted, they weren't supposed to, but Shade's limited dealings with humanity had, improbably enough, been solely with exceptions to the rule. She sometimes felt as if she were a character in a poorly written series of comedic novels and all her interactions with the human race were written largely for laughs (which she is, but because I think it would be in very poor taste to tell her so, let's just keep that between us, shall we?).

To test whether or not her impressions were correct, Shade took a tentative step forward and waved a hand at a toddler not much taller than her being led down the street by a kindly looking woman. "Hi, there, little . . . whatever you call a young human being. Hi."

The child paid her no mind and continued to toddle down the street, sucking on four of her fingers and drooling down her chin in that appalling way that parents always view as cute and the rest of the world knows is absolutely revolting. Encouraged by this, Shade called up to a portly gentleman strolling by, "Fwoo! I can't tell which smells worse—that stinking pipe or your feet!" Chuckling at his obliviousness, she turned to a sour-faced old woman hobbling along with a cane. "What's the matter, Granny? Been sucking on a pickle?"

In a blur of motion, the old lady's cane whipped over and clonked Shade on the head. "Ow! What the dangle?" Shade cried, clutching her head.

"Look, ya beut, just 'cause the rest o' this lot's too thick to see yez wee folk don't mean I am," the little old lady wheezed at Shade as people nearby looked at her like she was crazy.

Before Shade could reply, Ginch and the Professor dodged through the crowd to her side. "Whatta you do—runnin' off like that?"

"Ee, more wee deadbeats," the old lady grumbled.

"Say," Ginch said, straightening his tie and his eye patch and giving the little old lady his most winning smile. *"Mia bella nonna!* You would no happen to know where we find the Bowser twins or the secret book guys or—"

Shade punched his arm. "Stop asking people that! It's not going to—"

"Oh, I expect doon 'round the docks. That's where all the worst fairy folk seem to be. Now clear oot and mind yez manners."

Ginch blew her a kiss, which made the old lady scowl, although her cheeks did redden slightly. The three headed toward the waterfront, careful to avoid any humans. As they got closer, the air smelled more and more of fish and sea salt. Shade's stomach tied itself in knots. She was both excited to come closer to realizing her father's goal and afraid that she wouldn't be able to or that something might happen to her and her friends along the way. *And how exactly am I supposed to find twin gangsters and the headquarters of a secret criminal empire?* she wondered.

"Hey, how're we gonna to find the twin gangsters and the headquarters of the secret criminal umpire?" Ginch asked.

"I'll figure it out," Shade said. "We just need to look around the docks, ask a few questions—*me*, not *you*—and I'm sure we'll track down the Bowsers."

Ginch and the Professor twirled around and stopped, blocking her path. "So we look around, eh?"

"Yes."

"You think-a you figure it all out?"

"*Yes*," Shade said with more conviction than she felt.

Ginch and the Professor exchanged a doubtful look. The Professor reached into his coat and pulled out a pair of pants with a scroll sticking out of the back pocket labeled "Diploma." He handed the pants to Shade, bowed, and gestured for her to walk past him.

"The Professor says if you the smarty pants, then lead-a the way. Where we go?"

"Um . . ." Shade could feel her face getting hot. She hadn't expected to be called out like this, and she didn't like it, especially since she didn't have an answer. After spending her childhood as a reader and knowing much more than the average Pleasant Hollow sprite—not that that is saying much—Shade had become rather vain about her intelligence and hated to admit when she came to the limits of it, and she was clearly at a limit.

"You no know, do you?" Ginch smirked.

Shade pointed her finger at him and opened her mouth to say something profoundly insulting when the cry of a seagull made her look past him. What she saw made her smile. "Yes. Yes, I do know where we go. We go there!"

12

In which we learn that legitimate businesses do not need to note that they are, in fact, legitimate businesses . . .

Sometimes in life when we don't know where to go or what to do, we hope some power in the universe will send us a sign, like when your father was just out of school and wasn't sure what to do with himself and happened to spot a pamphlet on eel farming, which was his first step on the path to owning and operating the sixth largest eel farm in the country. Or the time when your Uncle Vernon looked down from a departure screen telling him that his flight to Lagos had been delayed to see a lovely barista at the airport coffee shop looking over at him as she served a plum Danish to a customer, thus beginning his great love affair with plum Danishes.

Similarly, just as Shade was almost forced to admit that she didn't know something, she spotted a very fortuitous sign. In this case it was an actual sign posted at fairy-height next to a fairy-sized door in the side of a run-down human tannery. The sign read:

Perfectly, Innocent, & Legal
Imports and Exports, Ltd.
A legitimate business and not at all
a front for a secret criminal empire.

"Whatta you mean we go there? That's-a the legitimate business, not the secret criminal umpire," Ginch said. The Professor nodded and pointed. "See—it says so on the sign."

Shade's brow furrowed. "What legitimate business would have to state that it's a legitimate business and not secretly a bunch of gangsters?"

"Why, every time the Professor and I go into the business, we tell people that we're legitimate. It's whatta you do in the business world. Right, partner?"

The Professor nodded and pulled out a series of business cards declaring Ginch and the Professor to be "Legitimate and Not at All Fake or Crooked" pony traders, fireworks experts, clockmakers, home security consultants, wedding planners, royal surgeons, cake tasters, rat catchers, chimney sweeps, attorneys-at-law, and finally "Purveyors of Post-Theft Items."

"But you two *are* fake and crooked when it comes to all of these . . . except that post-theft one."

"Yeah, but we make the cards *because* that's-a what the legitimate businesses do . . . We think."

"Just shut up, blabberbrownie, and come on!" Shade grabbed each by the arm and hauled them over to the store.

Inside was a small, dimly lit space crammed with decorative masks and Persian rugs, strange figurines and odd weapons, silk robes and straw hats, multicolored vials and jars filled with pickled creatures, flutes and drums and all manner of string instruments, and no end of gewgaws, gimcracks, and whatchamacallits. Perched on a stool behind the counter was a wizened fairy with a long gray beard full of tangled knots. He absentmindedly twirled a lock of it, creating a new knot in the process, while writing in a logbook when the tinkle of the bell above the door made him look over. The movement of his beard suggested that he was smiling at them but they couldn't tell because it completely covered his mouth. "Ah, customers! Delightful!" a muffled voice exclaimed from the depths of his facial hair.

As he hopped down and scurried over, Shade whispered, "Let me do the talking."

Ginch gave the Professor's arm a swat. "You heard the little Sprootshade. Dummy up and give somebody else the chance to talk!"

The Professor pretended to lock his mouth shut. As he mimed dropping a pretend key in his pocket, he did a double-take, then pulled out a lollipop, fuzzy with pocket-lint, which he popped into his mouth.

"So, messieurs and mademoiselle, what may I help you find this fine day?" the bearded fairy asked, clasping his tiny hands in front of his long beard.

"Are you one of the owners?" Shade asked.

"*Oui.* I am Monsieur Légal. I handle the day-to-day while my partners, Messieurs Perfectly and Innocent, scour all Elfame and her outer isles for the finest, most exotic, and most legitimate and legal imports."

"Sounds like a fascinating yet completely legitimate and legal line of work," Shade said.

"*Oui!* It is, it is."

"And not at all a front for a secret criminal empire."

"Oh, no, no, no! Of course not. That is why we have the sign, you see."

"Of course. But if someone were . . . maybe . . . interested in imports or exports that weren't *completely* legitimate and legal, you wouldn't happen to know who she could talk to, would you?" Shade gave him a wink.

The lutin's eyes narrowed and he nodded in a knowing manner. "Well . . . I might, perhaps, know of someone who might be able to help such a person," he replied, tapping the side of his nose with his finger, "if, say, you know of such a person who might be interested in such things."

"Oh, I believe I just might know of such a person." Shade winked again.

"What's-a the matter? You gotta something in you eye?" Ginch asked.

"Shush!" Shade hissed at him.

"If you know such a person, then I believe I know someone who could help." The hairy fairy again tapped the side of his nose.

"'Ey, you keep a-tappin' you nose. You gotta the cold?" Ginch asked. The Professor offered a filthy handkerchief to Monsieur Légal.

"Put that disgusting thing away." Shade slugged the Professor in the arm. "I'm sorry about these two."

The shopkeeper dismissed her apology with a wave. "Do not worry about it. The muscle—they never seem to understand the fine points of the business, no?"

Ginch laughed. "'Ey, partner—he thinks we're-a the tough guys!"

The Professor nodded and struck a series of body-builder poses.

"You might want to replace those two," Monsieur Légal said to Shade.

"You have no idea."

"So, what sort of less than legal items might someone you know be looking for?"

Shade shook her head. "I'm afraid I can't talk to you about that. Now if, let's say, this shop were a front for a secret criminal empire—"

"Which it is *not*. The sign and all . . . "

"Which, of course, it is *not*," Shade agreed. "But if it *were*, then I believe I could tell the boss of that criminal organization herself. Or themselves. As the case may be."

The hairy fairy squinted at Shade, sizing her up. "If this place were such a place and I were to introduce you to such a person, I would need some sort of guarantee that you could be trusted enough to meet with such a person."

"Oh, that's-a easy," Ginch said with a shrug. "We're-a the good, good friends of Ronnie the Bowser."

Monsieur Légal's eyes widened and Shade whirled around. "What the dingle-dangle are you doing?" she growled.

"You are the friends of Ronnie Bowser?" the lutin asked, sounding more than a little surprised.

"Yeah, sure," Ginch said breezily, looked down at his fingernails. "We have the weekly poker game. In fact, she owe me and my partner three—" The Professor shook his head and held up six fingers. "I mean, she owe us the six gold coins from our last game."

"Hang on," Monsieur Légal said, taking a stocking cap with a feather attached to each side out of his pocket. He put the hat on and immediately vanished.

"I said to let me do the talking," Shade growled through gritted teeth.

"And you talk and you talk and you talk, but you

and beardsy no do the nothing. I talk and we get things a-movin'."

Shade put her hands on her hips. "And *are* things 'a-movin'? Because at the moment, we are exactly where we were before except the person who may have been able to help us has just disappeared because you couldn't keep your mouth shut."

Suddenly, one of the cases of trinkets lining the walls swung out and from behind it strode a spriggan, fully inflated, his head almost touching the ceiling, his brown leather jerkin studded with pebbles and stones. Next to him walked a hulking, leather armor-clad human, almost as tall as the spriggan, with a squashed nose and close-cropped blond hair. On every finger, he wore a large ring shaped like a skull.

"So you lot're friends of Ronnette Bowser, then?" the spriggan asked.

"She's like the sister to us!" Ginch declared before Shade could stop him. The Professor pointed at Ginch and nodded in agreement.

"Roight, then," the spriggan said, giving them a grin that showed off his jagged teeth. "Come wiv us."

The human bowed slightly and gestured toward the hidden doorway they had just come through. "If yez please," he said.

"See?" Ginch hooked his thumbs in his vest and started walking. "Like I say—I get things a-movin'!"

13

In which things get a-movin' . . .

On the other side of the hidden doorway, Shade and company found a vast open brick warehouse filled with fairies—mostly goblins and hobgoblins, but also gnomes, dwarves, trow, pechs, spriggans, wulvers, kobolds, pixies, and even a troll—hauling boxes and rolling barrels right and left. The spriggan pointed to a metal door in the far wall.

"That way to the bosses' office," he said, leading them across the room.

On their way, a little man with flaming red hair and green overalls stumbled up to them, a tall glass of amber liquid in hand. "Evening, lads," he slurred, holding out the glass to them. "Fancy a tipple with me and me boys, Mr. Yaxley? Mr. Ront?"

"Can't," the human replied. "No bevvies when we's on the clock, la."

"This batch still taste loike paint thinner, Seamus?" the spriggan asked.

"Aye, Mr. Ront, but in a good way." The clurichaun drained the glass in one mighty gulp, then stumbled off.

"Make sure yez don't drink the whole batch, la!" Yaxley called after him. "We got to keep an eye on him, Ront. He's gettin' to be a proper deadbeat."

A badger-headed goblin rushed over holding up a footstool whose legs waggled of their own power. "Mr. Yaxley, what am I supposed to do with these bloody dokkaebis? They're runnin' all aboot the bloody warehouse sayin' the rudest things to everyboody."

"Be careful wiv 'em, Buck. Them posh Seelie Court swells think talkin', movin' furniture's dead fashionable right now and are willin' to pay for it."

"Hey, you big, ugly human git! Is that your head or did your neck just throw up?" the footstool squeaked. "Gah! I've seen better-looking heads on boils! Why, I bet your mother—"

Yaxley yanked the footstool away from the goblin, clamped it in his armpit, and grabbed one of the legs. "Don't," he said and then snapped off one leg. "Talk." Snap! "Aboot." Snap! "Me ma." Snap!

"You miserable brute! You horrid savage! You filthy, nasty—"

The footstool's insults were cut short when Yaxley snapped the now legless piece of furniture in half on his knee.

"Here." Yaxley shoved the broken remnants into Buck's arms. "Any moor o' this furniture gives ya lip, la, you joost show them that and say there's moore where it coom from."

"Thanks, Mr. Yaxley!" The goblin sauntered away, whistling happily.

"Is that always how you handle problems?" Shade asked, more than a little disturbed by the casual violence she had witnessed.

"Nah. Sometimes 'e ain't so gentle, roight, Yax?" Ront laughed as Yaxley cracked his knuckles.

"I hope you're paying attention to all this, Mr. Get Things A-Movin'," Shade whispered to Ginch, who gulped and tugged at his collar.

"'Ang on," Ront said when they reached the metal door. He rapped rhythmically—Shade could tell it was some kind of code—then opened the door. Yaxley bowed and motioned for them to enter. "After you, lady and gents."

A chill ran down Shade's spine. She had a very bad feeling but didn't see any other alternative. That feeling was completely justified by the rat-, frog-, and gull-headed goblins hiding on either side of the doorway who grabbed them as soon as they entered. The three friends struggled and thrashed and swore, but it was no use—they were outnumbered and overpowered. The goblins forced the three onto wooden chairs and tied them up.

"Let us go, you thistlepricks!" Shade shouted.

"Hang on." Yaxley stooped to pick up the eye patch the Professor had lost during the scuffle. "Why Ront, I do believe these soft lads is duplicitous."

Ront gave him a quizzical look. "Do-what now?"

"Duplicitous. You know, they was tryin' to poot one over on oos."

"I 'spect yer roight there, Yax. But they made one crucial mistake, they did."

"They shoor did, Ront." Yaxley grinned at them. "Yez let slip that yez is friends with Ronnie Bowser."

"And Ronnie, seein' as she don't loike people on general principle, the only friends she's willin' to 'ave is the two of us—"

"Which yez ain't."

"Thornburgh—"

"Which yez ain't."

"And 'er sister, Ginnie."

"Which yez ain't." Yaxley cracked his knuckles menacingly. "I believe yez is coppers' narcs lookin' to infiltrate oos. Or maybe spies for anoother gang lookin' to muscle in on our operation."

"Wait!" Shade shouted. "Okay, we don't really know Ronnie Bowser. That's just something that turnip-head made up. But we're not spies or informants or anything. We have urgent, secret business with the Bowsers and they would really, really want to see us if they knew about it."

"That's-a true," Ginch agreed. "Not the turnip-head part, but everything else."

Yaxley studied Shade. "Know what, Ront? I believe the li'l sprite."

Ront cocked an eyebrow as Shade let out the breath she had been holding, relieved. "You do, Yax?"

"I do. He's a turnip-head if ever I saw one."

Shade groaned.

"Roight ya are, Yax. Nick, go fetch us Tickler, then," Ront told a rat-headed goblin who scurried off.

"Now the rest of you sods need to bugger off. What's gonna 'appen in 'ere ain't gonna be pretty. Not pretty at all."

The goblins turned pale and rushed out, elbowing each other to get out of the room. As soon as they had cleared out, Nick dashed in, handed Ront what appeared to be a long sword sheathed in a well-oiled leather scabbard, its bronze handle polished and gleaming in the light, and dashed out.

"A work of art, Tickler is. Ain't she, Ront?" Yaxley shook his head in admiration.

"Absolutely roight, Yax," he agreed, offering him Tickler handle first. "How 'bout you do the honors, mate?"

"Ta. Don't mind if'n I do, la." The human took the handle and grinned malevolently at Shade, Ginch, and the Professor. "Now then, which one of yez wants to tell oos who yez workin' for?"

"I told you, saphead, we're not working for anyone!" Shade protested.

Ront sighed. "Aw, Yax. I do believe we's gonna 'ave to do this the 'ard way."

Yax tried to look sad but couldn't manage it and chuckled. "Good. Let's see what Tickler can tickle oot 'o these muppets."

14

In which we see what Yax can
tickle out of our trio . . .

"Wait!" Shade shouted. "We're not working for anyone! You can't do this!"

Yaxley, who had been about to unsheathe Tickler, stopped. "Hang on. The li'l sprite's got a point there, Ront."

"She do?"

"Yeah. We can't do this. Not with their shoes still on we can't. Geddem off, will yez?"

Ront laughed. "Roight you is, Yax."

When the spriggan reached for Shade's leg, she tried to kick him in the head but missed by inches. He grabbed her by the ankle and yanked her boot off. "Got a bit o' spirit this 'un, Yax."

"That she do, Ront. Now, who should I start on?"

Shade looked at Ginch and the Professor. "Leave them alone," Shade said. "They don't know anything. I'm the one you want."

"'Ey, that's-a no true!" Ginch objected. "None of us know the nothing, but they know more of the nothing than I do, so you let-a them go and do whatta you want to me."

The Professor whistled, shook his head "no," then waggled his eyebrows and blew a raspberry at the goons. Yax nodded at him. "I believe yez is the winner, la. Boot don't worry—these other two will get a front-row seat for what I do to yez."

"Leave him alone, snotbucket!" Shade shouted as she struggled to free herself from the chair.

"And why would I do that? This here's me favorite part of the job," Yax said, grinning.

"And 'e's an artist at this, 'e is," Ront added.

"That I am, mate," Yax agreed. "See, Ront here—he's a good bloke but hasn't got no finesse when it cooms to this."

Ront chuckled. "'E's roight, 'e is. Oi always go roight to the belly. No style, no art to it."

"He gets too eager, he does," Yax said. "See, once yez is at the belly, yez doon. No place to go from there. Me? I start with the toes. Good place to start, the toes. Most fairies break by the time I get to the li'l piggy, and if they don't, well . . . plenty of places to go froom there, la. Boot enoof talk—time for the Tickler."

Shade gasped as Yax grabbed the scabbard in one hand and pulled the handle out with the other. And then she was confused. "What's that?"

Yax gave her a toothy, menacing smile. "It's Tickler."

"I thought it'd be a sword," Shade said, nodding at

the long ostrich feathers attached to the sword hilt. "Ginch?"

"Yeah, I woulda bet the big, big money it was-a the sword," he agreed.

Ront and Yax looked at each other in bewilderment and annoyance. "It's called 'Tickler,' yez beuts," Yax said.

"Yeah. What, you fink we're gonna tickle you wiv a sword?" Ront scoffed. "'Ow'd that work, then?"

"Right yez is, Ront. I mean, if this were named 'Slashy' or 'Stabby McStabberton' or soomthin', then, yeah, 'course it's a sword."

"Well, naturally Stabby McStabberton's a sword. Wouldn't make sense otherwise."

"That's exactly what I'm sayin'."

"And you're . . . going to tickle us with that?" Shade asked, smirking.

"That 'e is. That 'e is." Ront pointed at Yaxley and laughed evilly. "And 'e won't stop until ya tell us 'oo yer workin' for or 'e drives ya insane."

"Maybe both." Yaxley threw his head back and laughed.

"'Ang on, mate," Ront said and then whispered to him, "Don't say that you'll keep ticklin' 'til they's crazy, Yax. If they fink you'll keep on ticklin' after they spill their guts, they moight not talk. You gotta make 'em fink they'll be done if they tell us what we need, roight?"

"That makes a lot o' sense. Ta, Ront," he whispered back. "As I was sayin', we'll tickle yez until yez talk *or* yez go crazy. But not both. Startin' with the pixie."

The spriggan yanked the shoes and socks from the Professor's feet, and Yaxley began vigorously tickling the Professor's toes with his ostrich feathers. Now, I know that having one's toes tickled doesn't sound like that bad of a fate, but take a moment to consider the time your cousin Nefertiti tickled you so badly that you nearly wet yourself after you had threatened to tell Neville St. Claire that Nefertiti had been writing his name surrounded by hearts in her school notebook. As bad as that was, Nefertiti was an amateur tickle-torturer and not a pro like the one Shade and company faced. Yaxley tickled and tickled and tickled the

Professor's toes with ever increasing speed and savagery, but the Professor, as I'm sure you would expect, made no noise, though his eyes watered and he squirmed like a worm headed for the fishhook.

"That's-a no gonna get the word outta him," Ginch said after about fifteen minutes of solid tickling.

The human stopped and shook out his arm, while the Professor caught his breath. "Is right, la. Guess it's time to take it oop a notch."

"Ginch?" Shade said.

"Yeah?"

"Stop helping."

"Get 'is ears, mate," Ront suggested.

Yaxley did just that, tickling the Professor behind each ear. When the pixie still remained silent, the spriggan untied the Professor's hands from the chair and held them over his head while Yax attacked the pixie's armpits with much alacrity. Soon the human was panting with exhaustion, yet the Professor made no noise.

"Right . . . yez bloody pixie . . . I'm through playin' 'round . . . "

Ront frowned. "That mean it's toime for—"

Yaxley nodded. "It is, mate. Lift oop his shirt."

Ront did, exposing the Professor's pale belly. With a growl Yaxley furiously tickled it, putting all his previous efforts to shame. It was a tickling unparalleled in the history of ticklings and no doubt would merit its own chapter in Lady Giggleton de Teehee's book on that very subject, if she ever puts out a new edition. But it was all for naught—the Professor remained silent.

Eventually, Yaxley dropped Tickler. Its bronze handle clunked on the ground as he wiped sweat from his very distraught face. "I can't . . . He's not . . . "

Ront gave an appreciative whistle. "We've finally met a nut ya can't crack, Yax. Oi never would've—"

The door to the office swung open before Ront could finish and there, in the doorway, stood . . . nobody. And then there was a squelchy sound, as if someone were walking in old, waterlogged sneakers.

"What's that sound?" Shade asked. Ront's and Yaxley's eyes got big, and the human held his finger to his lips to tell her to shush.

"What sound?" Ront asked, making a face at Shade as if to say, "Shut up!"

"I don't hear anything," Yaxley said.

"You don't hear that?" Shade asked. "That squishy sound? Like someone's walking around in—"

"Oh, coom bloody on!" a voice roared. Suddenly in the middle of the room there appeared a lean fairy standing a little over four feet tall, her long, jet black hair swept straight back from her severe blue face. Given what a well-read and knowledgeable Reader you are, I'm sure I don't have to note she was a skriker, one of the most fearsome fairies to stalk bogs, moors, and swamps. She wore a well-tailored, form-fitting, knee-length coat with fuzzy collar and cuffs made of what looked like black dog hair and a pair of expensive-looking black leather boots. "Yez could hear me?"

"Yep," Shade agreed. Ginch and the Professor nodded as well.

Yax sighed. "The boss is really sensitive aboot her feet," he whispered to them.

The skriker bent over a little so that her face was on

a level with Shade, Ginch, and the Professor. "Truth now—was it a slight squish or a loud squish? Like, how easy did yez hear it?"

"It was-a the pretty loud squoosh," Ginch said.

"Bloody cobbler elves!" she shouted, her voice becoming so shrill that everyone in the room's ears hurt. "I paid good money for these shoes, right? They said they'd keep me feet as silent as a cat what's had sneakin' lessons, they did. And do they work?"

"No," Shade said.

"NO, THEY BLOODY DO NOT!"

"Um, boss . . . " Yaxley said tentatively. "I think we got a situation moor important than yez shoes."

"Really? Well, maybe yez think that because yez don't get called a 'trash fairy' because yez have feet what make squishin' noises when yez walk!"

"Boss." Ront gently placed a hand on the blue fairy's shoulder as if he feared it might get bitten off. "These three said they're friends o' Ronnie."

"Noboody's friends with me sis except oos and Thornburgh, which these three ain't."

"Your sister?" Shade asked. "So you're Ginnie Bowser?"

"That she is," Ront replied.

"Best crime boss in all Elfame," Yax added.

"Boys even got me a moog what says so." Ginnie smiled and nodded toward a nearby end table where there sat a white coffee mug that read "World's Greatest Crime Boss."

"And boss—this pixie here?" Yaxley nodded at the Professor. "He's the hardest hardcase I've ever seen, boss. Me and Tickler couldn't get a peep oot o' him."

Ginnie Bowser walked over to the Professor and pointed a well-manicured black fingernail in his face. "I know this bloke." The Professor craned his neck and gave the finger a little kiss. The fur-suited fairy flicked him hard on the nose.

"Of course you do," Shade said, beginning to believe that everybody other than her somehow knew of the Professor's academic achievements. "Writer of *Pick a Pocket*, University of Streüseldorff lecturer, expert on intra-spatial studies and pure and applied pocketry . . ."

"Intra-pocket-what's-it? Never heard o' any o' that roobbish," the blue fairy said. "Nah, this bloke here? This is Loocky Pinky."

"Lucky Pinky?" Shade asked.

"Loocky bloody Pinky, the greatest smuggler in all Elfame."

The Professor blushed and batted his eyelashes.

"And he's the fairy what I paid quite handsomely to find and bring to me the Manx Cat ten soommer ago, and I ain't seen him since." Ginnie Bowser put her hands on her hips and glared at the Professor.

"The Manx Cat?" Shade asked. "I read about that in Tearling's *Believe It or Don't Because I Really Can't Be That Concerned with Every Reader's Credulity, Now Can I?* Isn't it one of the rarest treasures ever, and haven't hundreds of fairies died trying to possess it?"

"It is and they have," the boss fairy agreed.

"But I thought it was lost."

"Yeah, it was, boot Loocky here were supposed to make it not lost. So where is it, Loocky?"

The Professor looked thoughtful and somehow casually slipped a hand out of the ropes they were tied with and rubbed his chin. After a moment, he held up a finger and then plunged his hand deep into his pants pocket, the tip of his tongue sticking out as he fished around. After a moment, he pulled out a small obsidian statue of a tailless cat and handed it to the fairy, who lifted it up and smiled.

"Now that is beautiful, that is! Hang on." Ginnie walked over to the elegant oak desk in the center of the wood-paneled, bookshelf-lined room and put it on one corner. She took a step back, looked at it appraisingly, moved it to the opposite corner, considered it again, moved it an inch over, and gave it a quarter-turn. After another moment gazing at it, she finally raised up her hands. "There. What yez think, boys? I think it really ties the whole room together."

"Is right, boss," Yaxley agreed. "Gives it a whole new feel."

"Dead posh, that," Ront added. "Dead posh."

The boss fairy basked in her henchmen's compliments and then shook the Professor's free hand. "Right then, lads—how aboot you untie 'em. And what's all this rot about them bein' spies? Loocky here, he's a right lad if ever there was one."

"To be fair, boss," Ront said as he untied Shade, "that brownie did say 'e was friends wiv Ronnie."

"Oh, that was just the bluff," Ginch said, rubbing his freed wrists.

"And how did that work out for us?" Shade asked. The Professor held his nose, made a rude noise, and pretended to wave away a stinky odor. "Exactly. We don't know you or your sister—well, I guess 'Lucky' there does—but we know you're both part of G.L.U.G."

Ginnie Bowser's eyes narrowed. "And how do you know that?"

"Because I'm a member too. My great-grandfather worked with Máire Bowser in the Great Library."

"Granny Máire?" Ginnie asked.

"Yes. And we know that you and your sister have one of the codebooks that will reveal the hidden location of the library's lost books. We're trying to get all the book guardians together and bring Alexandria's books back to the world."

"Shoot the door, Ront," Ginnie ordered. As soon as it was closed, Ginnie let out a long breath and smiled. "A fellow G.L.U.G.er? That's brilliant! Boys, we can finally drop the act."

Yaxley and Ront smiled and gave each other a high five. "Looks loike we're out o' the villain game, Yax," Ront said.

"What act?" Shade had no idea what was going on.

"And what happen to you accent?" Ginch asked

"Oh, my sister and I adopted fake Bilgewater accents just to sound tough," Ginnie said, all trace of her former accent gone. "One loses a tad bit of credibility as a fake crime boss when one sounds too genteel."

"You use the fake accent?" Ginch shook his head. "Oh, the world, what do she come to?"

Shade rolled her eyes. "Hers was better than yours, you old fraud." The Professor nodded and pulled out a blue ribbon that he handed to Ginnie while Ginch pouted. "And what's this about being a fake crime boss?"

"Just what I said. Ronnie and I created S.H.U.S.H. as a front to hide the fact that we were in a secret society dedicated to protecting books and to try to get word of where the rest of you were. Kind of got the idea from our codebook."

"S.H.U.S.H.?" Shade said.

"Yes, S.H.U.S.H.—the Surreptitiously Honorable Undercover Society."

"What about the second 'h'?" Shade asked. "What's that stand for?"

"It doesn't stand for anything," Ginnie admitted. "But what kind of acronym would S.H.U.S. be?"

"Not a good one, that's for shoor," Yaxley said.

"S.H.U.S.? Bleh." Ront made a face.

"Exactly my point," Ginnie said. "I mean—"

"Look, I don't care about dingle-dangle acronyms," Shade interjected. "Somebody is trying to hunt us all down, so get your codebook and come with us."

"It's not here," Ginnie said.

"Then where the donkle is it?"

"Ee, lass! You kiss your ma with that mooth?" Yaxley asked.

"Shut it, goon! Where's the book?"

"Relax," Ginnie said, patting Shade on the back, which Shade did not at all care for. "We've got it secured in a secret safe house a few blocks away. Let me just take care of a few things here and then we can go get it and finally fulfill Gran's dream. Oh, she'd be so proud!"

Suddenly, loud crashes and shouts came from outside. Someone pounded on the office's metal door. "Ms. Bowser! Yez gotta get oot, boss! We's bein' raided!"

15

In which a safe house turns out
not to be all that safe . . .

The instant the word "raided" was shouted, Ront
hustled to the bookcase on the wall opposite the
metal door and pulled on a book entitled *A
History of Secret Passages and Hidden Exits*. The bookcase swung out to reveal a dark, windowless passageway.

"Raided?" Ginnie's face darkened and a vein bulged

on her forehead. "We're being *raided*? We control the police in Bilgewater!"

Yaxley put a hand on Ginnie's shoulder. "Boss, that don't matter right now. We just gotta get yez oot of here before the bizzies snatch yez."

"The human bean's right," Ginch agreed. "We gots to—"

"Skeedeedle?" Shade finished.

"'Ey, how you know what I'm-a gonna say before I say it?"

"I must be psychic," Shade said. "Now let's skeedeedle!"

Shade, Ginch, and the Professor (who paused a moment to grab the cat statue off the desk and stuff it in his coat) dashed into the dark passage. Yaxley followed, his hands massaging Ginnie Bowser's shoulders as he urged her onward, with Ront bringing up the rear. He pushed one of the bricks and the bookcase swung back into place, plunging them all into darkness that was quickly illuminated by a lit candle the Professor pulled out of one of his pants pockets. Ront pushed his way to the front and led them down a long, winding, cobweb-filled passageway that abruptly terminated in a brick wall.

"Knox," Ront said, and the bricks withdrew themselves one by one from the wall and formed a neat square pile. Shade, followed by everyone else, stepped out into a narrow alleyway. The moon was a blurry glow up in the foggy night sky, and the air was filled with shouts and cries and the sounds of breaking wood and metal clashing against metal.

"Wait here," Shade said before flying up into the air and over the roof of the tannery. One end of the alley led to the front of the building where the long-bearded lutin, Monsieur Légal, the tipsy clurichaun, and other fairies from Ginnie Bowser's warehouse were being hauled off by elves, dwarves, and goblins wearing bronze armor and green tabards with white roses. Shade flew to the other side of the building to find a series of alleyways branching off from the one on the side of the old tannery, all of which seemed to be empty aside from the occasional rat.

"This way," Shade said when she landed next to the others. "Seelie soldiers are arresting everyone they can grab on the other side."

Ginnie Bowser clenched her fists. Ront and Yaxley put their hands on her shoulders. "Boss, we need to—"

"I know what we need to do," Ginnie growled through gritted teeth. "But it boils my blood that there's a rat out there somewhere that won't be getting its comeuppance. Now let's get to that safe house. We'll get the book, lie low a bit, and then find my sister."

The six wound their way through shadow-shrouded, puddle-filled alleyways, down grimy half-deserted streets where a few stray fairies wandered muttering to themselves, past one-night cheap hotels and sawdust restaurants with piles of smashed oyster shells littering the sidewalks, until they came to an especially dark, run-down street whose signpost read "Prufrock Lane." Ginnie led them to a small house that looked to be the worst house in what seemed likely to be the worst neighborhood in town. Its sagging roof was green with moss, its dingy gray walls on the verge of collapse, and all its windows and front door were boarded up. "Here we are," Ginnie said, leading them around to the back.

The house's back door, unlike the rest of the building, looked new, solid, and strong. Ginnie took a key out of her coat pocket and put it in the lock. She started to turn it, then stopped, leaned forward, and put her ear against the door. "It's unlocked and someone's in there," she whispered.

Ront and Yaxley signaled the others to stand back. Yaxley took a pair of iron knuckles out of one of his pockets and slid them on while Ront put his hand on the doorknob. They nodded at each other and then threw open the door. From between the two bruisers, Shade could see a troll on the other side of the door.

Now at this point, good Reader, the author of these dreadful fairy books has no doubt warped your impression of trolls by presenting you with that dandy gentletroll Chauncey X. Trogswollop in our previous book. Well, I'm happy to report that what Shade spied in the Bowsers' safe house was, in fact, a *proper* troll:

his mane of coarse black hair wild and uncoifed; his green-gray skin rough and unmoisturized; his long fingernails jagged and unmanicured; his boar-like tusks, one of which was broken to half the length of the other, grimy and unbrushed. As for his attire—tattered brown breeches and a filthy leather vest topped with a necklace made of bones—well, Chauncey might very well faint dead away at the sight of it. In one of his hands he held a long wooden club, the end of which was barbed with rusty nails.

Shade gave a startled yelp as the Professor and Ginch cowered behind her. Their escorts, however, all relaxed. "Gave oos a bit of a fright there, la," Yaxley said, taking off his iron knuckles.

"What are you doing here, Thornburgh?" Ginnie Bowser asked, pushing past the troll.

"Uh . . . well . . . " Thornburgh the troll looked back over his shoulder. "We were just . . . "

"Come on," Ginnie said to Shade, Ginch, and the Professor, who all dutifully followed her past the smelly troll into a cozy sitting room with high-backed chairs, a red velvet chaise lounge, and an elegant marble fireplace where a fire crackled.

In one of the high-backed chairs sat a skriker who looked almost identical to Ginnie except this one wore her hair bobbed and her long fur coat had white pinstripes and no fuzzy collar. In her hands, she held a book: *The Fairy Godfather* by Puzo di Corleone. She started at the sight of them.

"Ginnie, what are yez doin' . . . " She trailed off and her eyes widened. She leapt up and squishily stormed over to them. "Loocky Pinky! Yez got a lot o' nerve showin' oop after takin' me money and—"

The Professor held up a finger, then reached into his jacket and pulled out the Manx Cat. Ronnie Bowser snatched the statue from his hands, admired it for a moment, then placed it on a nearby end table. After shifting it around a couple of times, she stood back and gave a satisfied smile. "There. What yez think? I think it really ties the whole room together."

Shade groaned. "Look, we don't have time to dink around debating interior decorating."

Ronnie's face flushed. She stepped in front of Shade and glared at her, so angry that she didn't seem to notice the Professor pocketing the statue again. "And who do yez think yez is, coomin' in here and—"

Ginnie pulled Ronnie back gently. "It's okay, sis. She's a fellow G.L.U.G.er and she's getting us all together to find Gran's books. We can stop pretending to be gangsters . . . and you can finally drop the accent."

"Boot I like the accent."

"You know what? Speak with whatever accent you like," Shade snapped. "Tap everything out in code. I really don't give a dingle or a dangle how anyone here communicates—"

The Professor gave a thumbs-up, licked his palm, shoved it into his armpit, and began flapping his arm and making sounds so disgusting that I absolutely refuse to describe them.

Shade swatted the Professor on the arm. "Okay, fine, I give a dangle about communicating *that* way. The point is, we need to get your codebook—"

"Which we've got," Ginnie said, grabbing *The Fairy Godfather* from Ronnie, who objected with a sharp "Hey!"

"—and get out of here. As I told your sister, someone's trying to hunt us all down."

"And there's them Seelie troops what raided our ware'ouse," Ront added. "Oi bet they's on the lookout fer us now too. Yax, best go check the door, mate."

"Hang on a tick," Ronnie said. She pointed at Shade. "You've got one of the codebooks?"

"Yeah, I've got one. In fact, we've collected three."

"Three?" Ronnie arched an eyebrow at this and studied Shade's face closely. "Where yez keepin' 'em? And where's—"

"Bosses, we gotta move and it's gonna get oogly," Yaxley declared as he put iron knuckles on both hands and balled up his fists. "We got coompany."

"How the dangle did the Seelie troops track us here?" Ginnie demanded. Shade saw Ronnie and Thornburgh exchange a concerned look.

"T'ain't Seelie, boss. It's a red cap gang, toof-lookin'

blokes with soom real hard lads, probably lookin' for a hostile takeover of our rackets. Blue-haired elf looks to be callin' the shots."

Shade dashed to the door and peeked through its peephole to see around twenty assorted red cap-wearing fairies, all of them with hard, mean faces, gathered in the backyard. In the lead was the same elf who had chased them in Cottinghamtownshireborough. "How the donkle did she get to Bilgewater so fast?" Shade muttered under her breath before rushing back to the others. "It's them—the ones hunting the book guardians. Are there any other ways out of here?"

Ront shook his head. "Yeah, but don't make no difference. If these geezers is worth their salt, they'll 'ave already covered every way out of 'ere."

Ginnie nodded grimly. "Our best bet is to charge out that door, fight our way past, and run for it."

Ront and Yaxley rolled their shoulders and cracked their knuckles. "Ront, Thornburgh, and I'll go oot first, crack soom skulls, and smash through their line," Yaxley said. "The rest of yez make a break for it."

The troll looked toward Ronnie, who gave him a slight nod. The three bruisers crowded around the door. Shade, Ginch, the Professor, and the Bowser twins got behind them. "Good lads," Ginnie said, giving Thornburgh, the nearest to her, a pat on the back. "Go!"

Thornburgh, Yaxley, and Ront charged out the door, swinging fists and clubs right and left. Shade followed in their wake as goblins, hobgoblins, dwarves, trows, several spriggans, and an ogre threw themselves at the Bowsers' bodyguards. Bodies fell as the three cut a swath through the crowd of combatants until at last they made it to the edge. There they parted, Thornburgh shifting to the right and Yaxley and Ront to the left to make a path between them.

"Go!" Ront shouted as he grabbed a hobgoblin and threw him at the head of one of the enemy spriggans.

"Don't worry about oos—we can handle these softies!" A bloodied Yaxley cried, burying his fist in the face of a goblin who charged at him with an ax held high.

The rest, led by the Bowsers, ran through the gap created by the bruisers, but just before they were clear the ogre broke free from the melee, leapt directly in front of them, and let loose with a horribly loud and vile-smelling roar right in the face of the twins. When he was done, the two exchanged an annoyed look, then opened their mouths and let loose with a piercing shriek that made everyone around them cover their ears. The ogre cried out in pain and dropped to his knees. The twins each kicked out a booted foot that connected with the ogre's chin with a mighty crack. The ogre's head snapped back, and he fell backward, unconscious.

"That'll teach yez to get in a shoutin' match with a skriker, yez biff," Ronnie scoffed.

"No time to gloat, sis," Ginnie declared. "We're not safe yet."

The others took that declaration to heart and ran out into the dark alleys with red cap goons struggling to pursue them and Seelie troops amassed throughout the city. It is at this point, good Reader, that I must end the chapter. I know—you desperately want to know what happens next. Well, as narrator, it's my job to build suspense to make you want to keep reading. Granted, it is unfortunate that at this particular moment you do not have the time to read another full chapter since it is time for your glass spiel lesson (and I must say, your water-filled wineglass rendition of Chopin's "Heroic Polonaise" is really coming along nicely), but I'm afraid professionalism and narratorial craft demand a cliff-hanger. I'm sure you understand, but I offer my apologies nonetheless.

16

In which your narrator's favorite
character finally makes an appearance
criminally late in the story . . .

S hade, Ginch, the Professor, and the Bowser
twins barreled through streets, dodging past
the few oblivious humans strolling about, duck-
ing into alleys and backstreets, but no matter where
they went, always they heard the footfalls, clanks, and
cries of either red cap goons or Seelie soldiers. Her
heart pounding and lungs and legs aching, Shade at

last signaled the others to follow her into a cluttered alley.

As they huddled there, hidden amongst empty barrels and crates, they heard a large group of Seelie troops march past. "Split up," one of them commanded. "Three crews. Remember: two skrikers, a sprite, a pixie, and a brownie. And keep an eye on the skies in case the sprite takes flight—owl-patterned wings."

Okay, I know they were after the Bowsers, but how do they know about the rest of us? Shade wondered.

Exhausted and terrified of being caught and arrested, Shade had no answer, but the troops had given her an idea. "Okay," Shade panted as she struggled to catch her breath, "We're going to . . . split up . . . huff, huff . . . Bowsers . . . turn invisible . . . get yourselves and . . . your codebook . . . to the library tree . . . huff, huff . . . east of town . . . "

Ginnie nodded. "We know the way."

"Here—give oos yez codebook," Ronnie said. "We'll get it there safe."

"It's already there," Shade said.

"Is they all there?" Ronnie asked.

Ginch shook his head. "We still gotta the one to go get."

"Enough talk," Shade said. "I think the coast is clear. We'll go one way. You two turn invisible and go another. Don't worry about us—just get to the library and tell anyone who works there who you are and what you've got. That way, even if we get caught, you and the other G.L.U.G.ers can still find the books."

Ginnie smiled and gave her a wink. "She's a tough old bird, isn't she, Ronnie?"

"Actually, Ginnie, I think she's moor of a bootterfly. And she seems pretty yoong to me, truth be told."

"I was being metaphorical. I mean, honestly, Ronnie, you'd think—"

"Just get out of here." Shade stood up. The Bowsers vanished. As soon as the sounds of squishy footfalls faded, Shade turned to her friends. "Come on. This way."

"That's-a no good. I say we go this way," Ginch said, pointing in the opposite direction.

"But the troops marched that way," Shade said.

"Which means they're-a no gonna come back this way anytime soon. Trust me—I do the skeedeedle so much I should get-a the Ph.D. in applied skeedeedling."

The Professor pointed at Ginch and nodded. Then he took out and placed a flat, square mortarboard on Ginch's head, handed him a piece of parchment that read "Honorary Doctor of Philosophy, University of Streüseldorff," moved the tassel on the hat from the right side to the left, then shook Ginch's hand.

Ginch wiped a tear from his eye. "After devoting so much of my life to the skeedeedling, it's-a so nice to get the recognition that—"

"This way! And try to keep up," Shade said as she ran in the opposite direction from the way that Ginch had recommended. She heard the other two scramble behind to catch up and smiled to herself both for getting her way and for knowing, deep down, that she was making the right call. And she felt that way right up to the point when she rounded the corner and saw four Seelie officers at the far end of the street.

"Maybe now you trust me to make the skeedeedling decisions," Shade heard Ginch say behind her. "Quick—in here!"

Shade turned to see Ginch and the Professor running toward one of the few shops that still seemed to be open: a bright red storefront filled with wheels and baskets of cheeses. Written in elegant gold letters on the window was "Wensleydale's National Cheese Emporium." She followed them through the door, above which a little silver bell jingled. Behind the counter, the shopkeeper's chain mail-clad back was to them as he dusted the shelves. "Welcome to Wensleydale's," he said without turning. His boredom-filled voice sounded oddly familiar to Shade. "How may I be of service to thee, good cheese enthusiasts?"

"Okay, since he's-a the human, he should no be able to see or hear us. So we—"

"I know that voice!" The shopkeeper straightened up and whirled around to reveal the handsome, bearded face of the most wonderful, noble, and dashing knight in all of Elfame—a hero far too good to be relegated to supporting character status in such a dreadful tale as this one and to have his entrance buried so late in the story to boot! But then, why should my opinion matter? I'm only an internationally renowned narrator and winner of no less than four Blabby Awards. What do I know? (Actually, quite a lot, I must say!)

"Sir Justinian!" Shade gasped. "What are you doing here? Last time we saw you, you were off to tell the Seelie Court that the Sluagh were abducting human children to raise as warriors."

The pleasure that had filled Sir Justinian's face at seeing his old friends vanished. "The 'good' King Julius and his 'wise and honest' advisors dismissed my claims due to lack of evidence and accused me of trying to undermine the uneasy truce between the Seelie and the Sluagh. What's more, when I pressed the issue, the vile knaves stripped me of my knighthood and relieved me of my commission in service of the Seelie Court."

"Why, that's-a no good!" Ginch shook his head in disgust. "So why you work inna the cheese shop?"

"My half-uncle needed assistance in the shop so he

could focus more on the cheese-making. And since I had nothing better to do—"

Through the window, Shade spied Seelie troopers coming toward the shop. "I'm really sorry to cut you off, but you have to hide us! If we get caught, our quest—"

"A quest?" Sir Justinian's eyes lit up, as Shade hoped they would. "Say no more, my good Lady Shade! Quick, behind the counter with the three of you!"

Shade, Ginch, and the Professor dived back behind the counter and pressed their backs to it. The bell tinkled. "Now try to stay clear of the human," the lead guardsman said to the other troopers. "He'll probably think the wind blew the door open or something and—"

"There's no wind, good guardsmen," Sir Justinian said.

"How can—Justinian?" The soldier, whom Shade could not see from behind the counter, sounded shocked. And then amused. "Ha! The great Justinian? So is this the great quest you've undertaken since being booted from the service? Well, I must say the cheesemonger's apron is much better livery for you than—"

A slap sounded. "Hold your tongue, Quaeth. The least of this man's adventures puts the greatest of your pathetic accomplishments to shame. Sir Justinian, I don't know if you remember me, but we fought together once at—"

"At the Battle of Whispering Springs. I do remember you, good Sergeant Johandra. You fought honorably and well."

"I thank you for the compliment, and it's now Captain Johandra. But I'm afraid I'm not here to exchange compliments. We are in pursuit of dangerous fugitives: two skrikers, leaders of a dangerous criminal organization, and three of their top officers—a brownie, a pixie, and a sprite. If you have seen them, I ask you on your honor as a knight of the Seelie Court to tell us where they are."

In the brief silence that followed, Shade held her breath and closed her eyes in dread. She trusted and admired Sir Justinian, but his honor had been appealed to, and he was, above all things, an honorable man. What *would* he do?

"I'm sorry, good Captain Johandra," Sir Justinian answered, much to Shade's relief, "but I have seen no such fairies."

"Very well. I thank you for your time. Good night and fare thee well, good Sir Knight."

"And fare thee well, good captain."

The bell sounded once more and Shade, Ginch, and the Professor all exhaled. Ginch smiled and pointed up at Sir Justinian. "'Ey! I no believe it! You make-a the lie to save us."

Sir Justinian smiled winningly as he threw off his apron and strode across the shop to lock the door. "No lie was told, good Signore Ginch. First, the good captain invoked my honor as a knight of the Seelie Court, which I no longer am. Second, there are no skrikers about the place, unless they are invisible. Third, I was asked if I had seen a criminal sprite, pixie, or brownie, and I know by your fair actions and good hearts that you are no criminals."

"Actually, they are criminals," Shade said, to which the Professor nodded, one hand full of cheese that he was about to stuff down his pants, the other full of coins from the cash drawer.

"Yeah, but we're-a no organized," Ginch said, to which the Professor whistled and passed him a business card that read "This is to certify that Lucius Theodosius Pinky is a member in good standing of the Greater Elfame Chapter of the Amalgamated Union of Smugglers, Con Artists, Thieves, Cutpurses, Pilferers, and other Assorted Criminal-Type Individuals." "'Ey, you no tell me you were going to join the union. Now you make-a me look like the scab!"

Sir Justinian put on his blue surcoat with golden lion head rampant and strapped on his sword and scabbard. "Come, friends. Follow me! I have spent many a sleepless night longing for adventure. Grouse! Good, sweet Grouse!" Sir Justinian led them to a back room where his thin, shaggy-haired, teenage squire was stirring a pot of bubbling cheese. "We need no longer languish in comestible exile."

"But I like it here," Grouse groused. "I've been learning how to make cheese, I've got the time and the means to really work on my cooking skills, and right this instant I'm on the verge of creating the perfect cheese fondue mix. The. Perfect. Cheese. Fondue."

"No time for dairy dillydallying, my faithful sidekick—"

"I'm more of a reluctant squire than a sidekick," Grouse grumbled.

"—for we have a *quest* to embark on!"

"A *quest*? Dingle-dangle it straight to . . . For the love of St. Bartleby, who the—*You!*" Grouse whipped his long wooden spoon out of the cheese pot and gestured angrily at Shade, Ginch, and the Professor, splattering them with melted cheese. "You three again! I thought you just wanted to find that library."

"We did," Shade said. "But now we're on a book-related quest and—"

"Gah! Stop saying the 'Q' word! Do you have any

idea what it does to—"

"I'm sorry, good Grouse, but we have no time for good-natured banter—"

"There's nothing good-natured about this, you—"

"Time is wasting. Hitch up the horse. Fill the cart with our gear, cheese, crates, and barrels. We'll hide these good fairies in their midst, throw a tarp over them, and smuggle them out of town. From there, it's onward to—"

"He's going say 'adventure,'" Grouse muttered bitterly.

"ADVENTURE!"

Grouse trudged off to do as he was told. "I hate my life . . ."

17

𝒥n which many library books are

checked out . . .

After a short and bumpy cart ride, Shade found Ginnie Bowser waiting outside the library tree. "Who is that?" Ginnie asked, her eyes narrowed with suspicion.

"This is Sir Justinian and Grouse—they're friends of ours," Shade explained.

"I'm not," Grouse grumbled.

"He is when he's in a better mood," Shade clarified.

"Which I never am," Grouse muttered.

"Which he rarely is," Shade conceded. "Where's your sister?"

"Haven't seen her since she turned invisible." Ginnie snorted. "Ha! Get it? See, if she's invisible—"

"I get it," Shade sighed.

"But don't worry about Ronnie. We Bowsers know how to look after ourselves."

"That we do," Ronnie declared as she blinked into view and squished over to them.

"What took so long, Ronnie?" Ginnie asked. "I've been here fifteen, twenty minutes."

"Lost me way, Gin, since I couldn't see where I were gooin', what with bein' invisibule and all."

"That doesn't make sense," Shade said.

"Makes perfect sense," Ronnie replied. "Yez see, if yez invisibule, that means yez can't be seen, so naturally I wouldn't be able to see me way here."

"No, but if *you* are invisible, that doesn't mean that . . . You know what? I don't have the energy for this.

I'll find places for everyone to sleep in the library to-night and we can figure out our next move tomorrow morning."

•

Exhausted from the night's adventures, Shade slept so late that when she finally awoke, the library was already open and the rest of the staff on the job. "You still work 'ere, Flutterbutt?" Caxton growled as he carried a stack of books past.

Shade had just enough energy to mumble something rude as she continued to the dining hall where everyone else was finishing breakfast. Ginch and the Professor leaned back in their chairs, patted their bellies contentedly, and took turns belching as Grouse, looking pleased for once, enjoyed a bite of a crêpe and Sir Justinian practiced sword-fighting techniques in a far corner. At the center of the table sat Poor Richard with a Bowser twin on either side, Ginnie gazing at him in rapt attention and Ronnie looking rather bored. "My dear, you're up!" he declared as Shade made a beeline for the coffeepot. "I was just regaling our new arrivals with tales of their dear grandmother, one of the most shrewd and cunning fairies I've ever known."

"Shrewd and cunning—that was our Gran," Ginnie agreed lovingly.

"Yep," Ronnie said dully, flicking a blueberry off her plate.

Shade took a swig of her coffee, its heat and pleasant bitterness instantly perking her up. "How's Martinko?"

Poor Richard's face dropped. "The poison is slowly progressing, and its nature continues to elude us."

"I'm sorry. Keep at it. And speaking of keeping at it, we have one more codebook to track down. After telling me about the Bowsers, Martinko said 'Grigor's tomb.'"

Poor Richard nodded. "Yes. Grigor Byrrower, our chief archivist. A good fairy—a coblynau from the Hollow Hills—but very solitary and more than a bit paranoid about security, which I'm sure the burning of Alexandria's library did little to alleviate. Before we went our separate ways, he vowed to protect his book for the rest of his life and forever afterward. I thought he was just being dramatic but now I suspect he actually took it with him into the grave."

"Where do you think his tomb is?"

"Ah, I anticipated that very question." The cowlug reached into his jacket and pulled out a map, which he handed to Shade. "The Hollow Hills. No doubt in my mind. From what I remember and based on a little research I did last night, I've narrowed things down to four likely mine shafts. Now, exploring all of them will be dangerous—"

"Dangerous? Then why do we sit here idle? Let us be off so that we may spit in the eye of death and tweak the nose of calamity!" Sir Justinian cried, overjoyed. He raised his sword in the air. "Who has the mettle to join the good Lady Shade and myself?"

"Not me," Grouse grumbled. "I'm staying here."

"But good Grouse, my squire—"

"Don't you 'good Grouse' me. I'm still in mourning over the fondue I had to leave back in Bilgewater. You try to make me go and you'll be looking for another squire."

The Bowser twins looked at each other. "Oot in the coontry?" Ronnie asked. "We're city fairies, boorn and raised. I'll pass. Beside, think I'll goo back to Bilgewater and check on the business."

"Why?" Ginnie asked. "The criminal organization was just a front. We're done with it now."

"Well . . . I need to goo check in on the lads, though, don't I? We left Yax, Ront, and Thornburgh in an awful tight spot, sis."

"Good point," Ginnie agreed. "I'll wait here. Maybe Richard can tell me more stories about Gran."

A frowning Shade and beaming Sir Justinian turned to look at Ginch and the Professor. Ginch quickly looked up at the ceiling and started whistling; the Professor took out a nail file and began giving himself a manicure. Shade put her hands on her hips. "Guys?"

Ginch sighed and picked up a croissant. "Fine! Fatcha-coota-matchca, sproot! But first I'm a-gonna eat this because I no like to almost die without the full stomach."

The Professor nodded, then stuffed a sausage, three hard-boiled eggs, and half a cantaloupe into his pockets.

"Good. We'll leave in a few minutes. First, I want to see about something," Shade said as she got up from the table.

Shade found Johannes at the circulation desk, hunched over some paperwork. "Hey kitten-britches, did you find out anything about the books on that list?"

"Ja, I did," Johannes said, taking out a piece of parchment. "Very much interest in those titles this veek. Caxton and I have listed the names of all fairies who have checked out each title and noted vhen patrons whose names ve do not know have looked at the books in the library vithout checking them out. In all cases, ve have written vhich door each came through."

"Great work." Shade studied the paper. She had hoped to find one fairy going through all the books, one fairy working for Perchta or whoever was after G.L.U.G., that they could track back to their enemy. But not a single fairy had looked at more than a single book on the list. What's more, the readers listed came from all over Elfame. Disappointed and frustrated, Shade pushed the paper back to Johannes. "Oh, for the love of St. Eeyore . . . "

"The list is no good?" Johannes looked disappointed. "Perhaps ve—"

"Fetch the head librarians!" Grand Scrutinizer Drabbury shouted as he marched to the circulation desk from the door to Ande-Dubnos, a scroll clutched in his claws. The bugbear glared at Shade through his smoked-glass lenses, looking quite pleased with himself, rather more a "smugbear" than a "bugbear." "In the name of M.O.A.N., I demand to see them this instant!"

"Fetch them yourself," Shade fired back.

"If you insist on making zis racket every time you come 'ere, you may force me to teach you ze lessons on manners," François declared as he and Émilie came swiftly down. "Whether you prefer with ze book or with my fists, I am 'appy to accommodate."

"And what can we do for you today, Monsieur Drabbury?" Émilie asked.

The bugbear thrust the scroll at them. "First, you

address me by my title, 'Grand Scrutinizer.' And as you can see, both the Seelie and Sluagh courts have signed orders authorizing me to immediately confiscate any books I deem a clear and present danger to Elfame. Unless you want military garrisons to haul you and your staff out in chains and seal up every entry to this library, you will immediately order your staff to bring every copy of every book on these pages to me this instant." Drabbury slapped ten sheets of parchment onto the circulation desk.

"Listen, slug snot," Shade said heatedly, "if you think we are going to give you even one single book on that list—"

"Shade, please," Émilie interrupted. "I'm afraid we must."

"What? We can't just—"

"I am afraid we must," François said gently. "Ze orders say exactly what 'e says, and we do not want anyone arrested or blocked from ze library, *n'est-ce pas?*"

Shade looked with disbelief at the two librarians. *How can they just give up like this?* she wondered as a

deep anger born of having one's home threatened—
one of the deepest angers there is—began to well up
inside her. She balled up her fists; her face flushed.

Drabbury snorted. "What? Nothing to say now that
you know who is truly in charge here, little sprite?"

Shade walked over to the bugbear. As she was only
as tall as his kneecap, she was forced to look a long way
up at him. "You are a no-good, slug-licking, pond
scum-slurping pile of snake scat."

Behind Drabbury's dark glasses, his eyes flared and
the lenses glowed red. While she wasn't completely
sure, Shade thought she saw wisps of smoke curl out
around their edges. Under normal circumstances, she
probably would have been at least a little afraid of him,
but she was too furious just then to feel anything other
than rage.

Shade felt a cold, smooth hand on her shoulder, but
she refused to turn away from Drabbury. "Shade, this
is not helping matters," Émilie said. "The Grand
Scrutinizer will wait with us in our office while you
and other members of the staff go collect all of the

books on this list that haven't been checked out and bring them up, *s'il vous plait*."

That command did get Shade to turn away from Drabbury but did nothing to calm her. In fact, it enraged her more. "Give him the books? *Give him the books?* You seriously are going to hand over the books of this library to this—this—dingle-dangle-donkle dungball?"

"*Oui*," François said. He looked very serious but—and Shade wasn't sure at first because of how worked up she was—there was the slightest hint of a smile in the corner of his mouth and the slightest gleam of mischief in his eyes. "As Madame Tonnelier 'as told you, we need you to go and collect every *available* copy of ze books on zis list. If a book is 'ere and *not checked out*, we expect you to bring it to ze Grand Scrutinizer, *oui?*"

Shade instantly got the message and grabbed the sheet of papers. "Fine! I'll get the books, but—" she pointed her finger up at Drabbury's face, "you're still a pile of snake scat!"

As the librarians led Drabbury up to their office, Shade shouted, "I need all staff at the circulation desk right now! Especially you, Dewey! Justinian, Richard, Bowsers, Ginch, Professor—I need you too!"

Everyone came running, with Dewey bringing up the rear, his bowtie a touch askew and a single hair hanging slightly down on his forehead. "I'm sorry for my frightful appearance," he said, instantly straightening his tie and smoothing the hair with his hand. "I was in the weeds on the children's section and—"

"Sorry, Dewey, no time for all that." Shade handed him half the pages and gave the rest to everybody else. "Okay, we need to get every copy of every book on these pages off the shelves and checked out or else Norbutt Dungberry is going to confiscate them. Get them fast and bring them here."

"Okay, but who's gonna check out alla these books?" Ginch asked.

"You, the Professor, Poor Richard—everybody who doesn't work here."

"Can we help?" Shade turned to see the cloaked elfin kids standing behind her. "We'd really like to help."

Shade smiled and gave each some pages. "Absolutely. Now get cracking, everyone!"

Dewey ran from shelf to shelf, knowing by heart that week's organizational structure—smallest to largest calculated density of each book. The rest went to the card catalog, pulled out and tossed cards, then followed each card as it marched, sprinted, galloped, sailed, or flew to its corresponding book. They carried armload after armload to the circulation desk where the non-staff members took turns checking them out.

Once the last book was officially signed out, all of them were squirreled away in Johannes's book repair room. As the fairies and knight returned to the main floor, the Grand Scrutinizer strode down the central spiral with François and Émilie following behind. The head librarians looked at Shade, who gave them a nod. Both looked much relieved, and François took an extra-large sip of his ever-present coffee.

"I have waited long enough," Grand Scrutinizer Drabbury declared. "Where are the books? I am a busy fairy and have much to attend to. Hand them over, and I will be on my way."

Shade sighed and shook her head. "I'm so sorry, Grand Scrupelizer—"

"That's *'Grand Scrutinizer,'* young lady."

"Whatever. Anyway, I'm afraid that we don't have any of the books on this list."

Drabbury snorted. "You know that is a lie, girl. And one easily disproven."

The bugbear marched over to the card catalog, opened one of the drawers, and yanked out a card. "Right here: *The Terrific Jimmy Gatz.*" Drabbury held out the card for all of them to see. "One of the indecent books on the list—glamorizes a life of crime, major characters engage in lying and cheating, and other moral offenses—and here it is in your collections."

"Yeah, but Mr. Drudgery—"

"That's *'Drabbury,'* you little—"

"Whatever. As I was saying, we don't have it. Yes, it's in our collections, but it's checked out." Shade smiled and crossed her arms. "*All* the books on your list, it turns out, are checked out."

"I find that hard to believe. *Very* hard to believe." Drabbury tossed the card, but rather than fold itself into a stylishly dressed young elf and confidently saunter over to a bookshelf, the card did two loop de loops and refiled itself in its drawer. "Fine, perhaps that one is checked out but surely the others . . . "

Drabbury opened another drawer and pulled and tossed a card, which refiled itself just as the previous one had. He opened another drawer and another and another with increasing speed and force, and again and again the tossed cards went right back to their drawers. With a growl, Drabbury slammed the last drawer shut and whirled around.

Ginch gestured to the card catalog. "See, it's like she say, Mr. Booger-the-bear—"

"That's '*bugbear*,' you filthy, thieving brownie."

"'Ey, I'm-a no filthy. I take-a the bath . . . Hey, partner, when I take-a the bath?"

The Professor held up two fingers, then pulled a rubber ducky out of his pocket and tossed it to Ginch.

"I take-a the bath two months ago. And if you no believe me, you ask the duck." Ginch held the duck out to Drabbury and gave it a squeeze. It squeaked.

The bugbear swatted the duck from Ginch's hand

and rounded on François and Émilie. "If all these books are currently checked out, then I demand the names and whereabouts of all fairies currently in possession of them, which you will compile and hand over this instant."

François's eyes narrowed. "Zat is out of ze question. Only ze Grand Library's staff may see such zings. We do not share any information about our patrons."

Drabbury tilted his head back and looked down his nose at the librarians. "Then, by the authority vested in me by the Seelie Court and Sluagh Horde, I shall have all of you arrested and this library closed."

"I do not believe you will." Émilie held out the orders she and François had been looking at earlier. "According to these official orders, you are authorized to do that if we do not produce the books, which you see is currently impossible. They say nothing about confidential library records. If you go back and get authorization for those, then we can discuss that possibility."

"As ze officer of ze governments, I'm sure we need

not explain to you ze importance of official paperwork, non?" François took a sip of coffee to hide his smile.

"Yeah. Go push some papers around, Drudgery," Shade said.

Drabbury growled and raised his arm as if to stab Shade with his elbow barb but stopped himself and scratched at his chin as if that had been his intent all along. "Very well. I shall return with the necessary paperwork. I shall also note your reluctance to follow official orders—"

François shrugged. "We would be most 'appy to 'elp, but ze paperwork . . ."

"I shall also officially report the rudeness with which I have been treated while fulfilling the duties of my position."

"Oh, there was no insult intended, I'm sure," Émilie said soothingly. "Our page, well, she sometimes has trouble with names."

Shade grinned. "Oh, no. I was *intentionally* insulting this creep. Because, you know, he's a creep."

"Our business is concluded for now, but I shall return shortly and finish it . . . and possibly finish all of you." Drabbury turned on his heel and marched out the door to Dinas Ffaraon without a backward glance. Had he glanced backward, he might have seen the Professor sneak up and attach a sign to his back that read "Kick Me" with an arrow pointing down to his rear end.

Shade turned to Ginch, the Professor, and Sir Justinian. "So that's done. Now why don't we move on to something more pleasant, like maybe dying in a mine shaft?"

18

In which we learn the disgusting truth about unicorns . . .

Located on the eastern coast of Elfame at the southern tip of the Hollow Hills, Mamlwytho was a once bustling mining town. After fairy miners exhausted the deposits of copper, silver, and gold that once filled the now hollowed out hills (hence the name), Mamlwytho had gone back to being a sleepy little coastal town of fairy farmers and fishermen. Only the most tenacious miners were still at it, trying desperately to squeeze more wealth from the earth. The streets were quiet as Shade, Ginch, the Professor, and Sir Justinian stepped out of the branch of the library tree that grew in the center of town.

"All right," Shade said, studying the map Poor Richard had annotated for her. "We're here. It looks like the first site is due north of—"

"Psst! If you're fortune hunters, I can take you right to a cache of gold that will make you rich," a gravelly voice said.

Shade turned to see who had spoken, but all she could see was an old yellow mule, with an unruly shock of curly black hair between his big ears and an odd tuft of equally black hair just below his lower lip, hitched to a post outside a livery stable. "Who said that?"

"That would be me," the mule replied.

"You talk?" Ginch asked. "How come you can-a talk?"

Sir Justinian's eyes lit up. "No doubt this is some good wizard cursed by a rival who will provide fortuitous aid to us until we may restore him to his true form."

The mule cocked an eyebrow at that. "Uh . . . Yeah, why not."

"And whatta you say about the fortune?"

"I can take you to a secret stash of gold up in the hills that would make you richer than in your wildest dreams."

"I no know about that," Ginch said as the Professor shook his head. "We have-a the dream last week where we're the pretty rich."

"I can make you exactly three and a half times richer than that," the mule said. "All you have to do is buy me from the abusive jerk who runs this dump, and I'll take you there."

"It's-a the deal," Ginch said. The Professor patted the mule on the head, then took a handful of oats out of the feedbag hanging on the post next to him and started eating it.

"Wait. We're not looking for gold," Shade said.

"Speak-a for yourself!"

"Then what are you looking for?" the mule asked.

Shade leaned in. "The tomb of a coblynau named Grigor Byrrower."

"Oh, I've done supply runs up into the Hollow Hills for years. I can take you right to it—wouldn't take more than a couple of hours."

"And then you take us to the gold, and we get-a the money back and a lot more?" Ginch asked.

"And you'll become our boon companion in exchange for us eventually restoring you to your wizardly glory?" Sir Justinian chimed in.

"Yeah, sure. The gold, Grigor Byrrower, the wizard stuff—whatever you want. Just get me out of here before I get another beating."

Shade wasn't sure that she believed a single word the mule had said, but the thought of an animal being abused was enough to make her take a chance on him. And so Shade, Ginch, and the Professor soon rode into the Hollow Hills in a cart pulled by the mule who hummed as he walked, with Sir Justinian striding alongside.

"So, you gotta the name?" Ginch asked. "Or do we just call you the mule?"

"Trudgemore," the mule answered. "And for the record, I'm not a mule."

Sir Justinian's eyes gleamed with excitement. "I knew it! You really *are* a wizard."

"Nope. Sorry. Just played along with that to try to make the sale."

"Oh." Sir Justinian looked disappointed, then perked up. "Then surely you are some noble prince who's been transformed into a beast as poetic punishment for your 'beastly' behavior who must be kissed by a fair maiden like our good Lady Shade here to restore his humanity!"

Shade grimaced. "Um, ew, no."

"That goes double for me, bug girl," the mule said. "And, again, no. I haven't been turned into anything."

"But since you can talk, surely—"

"Oh, that?" Trudgemore rolled his eyes. "All horses, ponies, donkeys, and mules can talk."

"Then how's come I never hear the pony talk before?" Ginch demanded.

"I don't know. I think most are just too lazy to learn anything other than pony. Besides, your average pony is not the greatest conversationalist. Unless you want to talk about oats, water, and how nice it is to have your mane brushed, I wouldn't bother trying to strike up a conversation with one."

"So, good Trudgemore, if you aren't a mule, then what—"

"I'm a unicorn."

"A unicorn?" Shade smirked.

"A unicorn."

"You're not a unicorn. Where's your horn?"

"I was born without one." Trudgemore sighed. "Everybody always brings up the horn—"

"Well, it is *the* defining feature, after all. And aren't you supposed to be a horse instead of a mule?" Shade asked.

"Isn't the brownie supposed to be cleaning a house somewhere?" Trudgemore fired back.

"I no do the housework," Ginch said, shuffling some cards.

"And isn't the pixie supposed to be dancing and singing and mesmerizing people?"

The Professor blew a raspberry at the back of the mule's head before taking a handful of oats out of his pocket to chew on.

"And you're not flitting about a forest somewhere tossing acorns or whatever it is you butterfly people do, so there we go." Trudgemore snorted. "Look, just because my body doesn't match up with what I am on the inside doesn't mean I'm not a unicorn."

Shade still wasn't buying it. "Okay, then. Do some unicorn magic."

Trudgemore turned to look at Shade, his eyes so wide that the whites showed. He batted his eyelashes at her and whinnied. In spite of herself, Shade found it kind of cute. "Okay, so what was that?" she asked.

"We unicorns can make most girls and some boys fall in love with us."

"I didn't fall in love with you."

"Yeah. Most age out of that once they're forty-five,

fifty seasons old. I can also neutralize poisons, so I've got that going for me."

"Really? Because it says in Bea L'Eggle's book, *The Penultimate Magical Equine*, which is pretty authoritative, that unicorns do that with their horns."

"Never heard of this L'Eggle, but I bet they never met an actual unicorn in their life. No, we do it with our spit."

"Ew, gross." Shade made a face.

"Yeah, we'll see what you say if I ever have to cure you of a snakebite or make some water drinkable for you."

"I'm not letting you spit in my water."

"Well, I believe you," Ginch said, giving Trudgemore a pat. "You're-a the mulicorn."

"Finally." Trudgemore smiled or at least did the nearest thing to smiling that a mule can manage. "And it's 'unicorn.'"

Ginch grinned benevolently. "You can-a be anything you want as long as you take us to the gold."

"Oh, there's no gold. I just made that up to get out of there."

"Fatcha-coota-matchca, mule!"

"I figured as much," Shade said. "What about Grigor Byrrower?"

"Oh, that's gold—no pun intended." Ginch gestured rudely at the mule in response. "I really have done a bunch of supply runs. It's funny—these hills have been pretty dead for years, but suddenly it's picked way up."

"How so?"

"Somebody's hired a bunch of the old miners to start digging around the mines again."

"How recently?" Shade had an uneasy feeling in her stomach.

"Hard to say—your average equine doesn't have a really great sense of time. One thing I can tell you, though, is nobody's bringing any ore into town. Doesn't even sound like they're looking for precious metals—just digging for the sake of digging, if the local ponies are to be believed."

"Guys, are you thinking what I'm thinking?" Shade asked.

"That next time we need a horse we should try harder to find one that is really a cursed nobleman or wizard?" Sir Justinian grumbled.

"No."

"That we should go back and find the card game since we no have the secret treasure to find?"

"No."

The Professor held out a handful of oats toward Shade, who swatted them away.

"*No.* Whoever it is that's been hunting all of us G.L.U.G.ers down—I think they've beaten us here and are digging around to find the tomb. I think we could be in very serious danger."

Sir Justinian smiled. "Danger? *Serious* danger?"

"Yes."

"Ha-ha!" Sir Justinian punched the air joyfully. "Yes! We'll have a chance to look into the grisly maw of death! What say you, my boon companions?"

Shade sighed and shook her head. The Professor stuck his tongue out and threw a handful of oats at him.

"I think maybe I'd like to go back to the stable," Trudgemore muttered.

"All sales are final," Shade said. "Maybe a little *too* final . . ."

19

In which a character's offer to spit
is (mercifully) rebuffed . . .

In spite of her worries about running afoul of her
enemies and Trudgemore's tendency to hum and
sing sad songs, Shade was moved by the beauty of
the Hollow Hills. Miles and miles of hills stretched
out before her, most smoothly rolling from one to the
next like great waves on the ocean, others forming tall
peaks like wizards' hats, still others as round as gigan-

tic eggs. Dark caverns, looking like yawning, hungry mouths, gaped at their bases. What surprised and delighted Shade the most, however, were the colors and smells. She had expected lush green grasses to cover the hills, which they did, but she didn't expect the swaths of pink, purple, orange, and red honeysuckle, the crowds of yellow daisies and daffodils, or the bursts of violet, indigo, and white lilac bushes that painted the hills and perfumed the air.

"Pretty, ain't it?" Trudgemore said as he pulled them along a winding dirt path. "The view always did take a little of the sting out of forced servitude."

"Well, now that you're free, maybe you can enjoy the view even more," Shade said.

"Yeah, sure feels like I'm free, hauling you folks around. Not that I don't appreciate the fact that you aren't whipping me to make me go faster and all."

"Don't worry—we're not going to keep you. Just get us to where you think Grigor Byrrower's body might be, then back to town, and you're free," Shade said.

"I'll believe it when it happens. But for now, I'll hope you're playing straight with me and pick up the pace a little." Trudgemore broke into a trot.

The cart clattered through the hills as Shade luxuriated in the morning sun and the delicious smells of blooming flowers. Trudgemore eventually pulled them down through a deep valley lined with pine and spruce trees where a small waterfall splashed into a crystal clear pool of water. He took them to the pool's edge. "Here we are," he announced.

The fairies climbed out of the cart. "Is this water safe to drink?" Shade asked.

"Should be as sweet and wholesome as Grandma Molly's apple crumble," Trudgemore declared. "Want me to spit in it to be on the safe side?"

"No."

Sir Justinian looked around expectantly. "We came not here for refreshment, good unicorn. We came in search of adventure."

"We came in search of a *book*," Shade clarified.

"I was a-hoping for the hidden gold, but the mule lie

to us," Ginch complained. "Fatcha-coota-matchca, mule."

"First, thanks for acknowledging that I'm a unicorn, Mr. Knight. Not enough people are polite enough to do so." Trudgemore paused to glare at Ginch. "Second, look behind the waterfall. One of the old-timers—a really sweet pony named Zerelda—told me when I was just a foal about how she used to work for this crazy old coblynau named Grigor right up until he died and passed her on to this couple of coblynau he was friends with. He'd have her graze a couple hills over so's nobody would know where he lived."

"It's here!" Sir Justinian shouted happily from behind the waterfall. "It's here and it's glorious!"

"You might want to tell him to keep it down a little," Trudgemore said as Sir Justinian's cries echoed throughout the valley. "Those people digging up the old tunnels that you were worried about? They're working the surrounding hills. Haven't hit this one as far as I know."

"Hey, Sir Justinian!" Ginch yelled as the Professor

took out a pair of cymbals and smashed them together. "The mulicorn says to quiet down!"

"Come see, my good fellows! Come see!" Sir Justinian shouted, undeterred.

Shade unhooked Trudgemore from the cart and patted him on the nose. "Wait here for a little bit. We'll be back as soon as we get our book."

"Good luck. If I don't see you by night, I'll just assume you're dead and go on my way." Trudgemore started singing lowly to himself. "Oh, the roads run long, and the winds blow cold, and the moon hides her face in all her shame . . . "

Shade walked gingerly along the rocky ledge that ran behind the waterfall. There a mine shaft gaped, leading into the hill. A breeze blew out from its black depths, chilling Shade as she read the sign that had been driven into the loose gravel at its mouth: "Danger! Keep Out!" At the foot of the sign was a pile of yellowed bones with a cracked skull on top.

"Now *this* appears to be a challenge worthy of a knight errant," Sir Justinian said, taking one of a pair of unlit torches that hung on each side of the cave entrance. "Good Professor, have you something to light this torch?"

The Professor nodded and pulled a smoldering cigar from his pants pocket, gave it a few puffs to make the end glow orange, made a disgusted face, and lit the torch with the end. He did the same to the other torch for Shade. Then he pulled a lantern out of a pocket and lit it for Ginch, and then finally took a lit candle out from inside his jacket and began walking into the depths of the cave.

Shade gazed around as they made their way into the hill, winding their way along the underground tunnel. Water trickled down the rough-hewn, dark gray stone walls, which were reinforced by rotted, worm-eaten wooden beams. She reached out to test the strength of one; the part she grabbed crumbled easily in her hand. "That doesn't inspire confidence," she muttered.

The Professor gave a whistle. They had reached a fork in the tunnel. He squatted down and inspected the ground. The right branch was wider and the ground there was worn smooth; the left, narrower, its ground rougher, had no wooden support beams to reinforce the walls or ceiling. The Professor pointed to the right and started to walk but Shade grabbed his coat and yanked him back.

"No," she said. "The left. Think about it—if this Grigor guy was a crazy security freak, he'd probably hole up and hide his book in a less-used passage. We should also be on the lookout for traps."

"A shrewd thought, good sprite." Sir Justinian began to push his way past the others. "Allow me to lead the way, for I—"

"No," she said. "If this were a fight, I'd put you in the front. In fact, if we're going to get attacked, which has happened a couple times already, it would probably be from behind, so you should bring up the rear."

Sir Justinian nodded and drew his sword. Ginch chuckled and nudged the Professor. "She said 'rear.'"

Shade rolled her eyes. "Professor, you lead the way."

The Professor's finger shot immediately to the tip of his nose. "He says-a the not it," Ginch explained.

Shade grabbed the Professor and shoved him toward the tunnel. "Come on, pixie-pants. You're the quickest on your feet—" The Professor nodded and broke into a quick jig at this. "—so you should go first. You'd have the best chance of dodging anything that we might accidentally trigger. Don't worry—you'll be fine. Just be careful."

The Professor gave a thumbs-up and began skipping ahead of them carelessly, whistling as he went. "He's-a my partner, so if he dies, I call the dibs on his stuff," Ginch said, following after him. "Hey partner, slow down. I no wanna go too far to find-a you body, eh!"

20

In which our characters encounter
mostly family-friendly peril . . .

Their footsteps echoed in the tunnel. Torchlight flickered. The tunnel began to gradually widen and the four spread out, with Ginch joining the Professor in the lead and Sir Justinian and Shade a few steps behind. Shade scanned the passageway.

"This reminds me of one of my books growing up: *Sultan Suleiman's Mines*. This adventurer goes looking for lost treasure, and there are all sorts of traps like—hold on! Don't anybody move!" She held her torch over toward the wall. There she saw holes: rows and rows of holes with three-inch spaces between them starting about a foot off the ground and reaching up almost as high as the ceiling.

Ginch squinted at the wall. "What? The mine, it's gotta the termites?"

"No. There was something like this in the book. Somebody kicks a trip wire and a bunch of arrows shoot out. See how the holes in the—" As Shade stepped back to better point out the holes to the others, the rock under her foot sank down and she heard a soft click. "Everybody get down!"

Shade dropped to the floor and covered her head. There was a whoosh of air and an odd bubbling sound. She looked up and saw jets of bubbles flying out of the holes. The Professor sprang to his feet, smiling and clapping, bubbles flying around him. The others stood up as well.

"An odd form of trap," Sir Justinian said as the bubble jets abruptly stopped. He leaned in to regard one of the holes. "Not a terribly effective security measure, in my opinion."

Shade scratched her head and looked at the wall while the Professor bent down and pushed on a stone. "Yeah. Why would you—pft!" A stream of bubbles flew directly into her face. "Knock it off, Professor!"

The Professor, undeterred, pushed the stone down several more times, filling the tunnel with bubbles. As they popped, he walked further down and then stomped on another stone. Bubbles again jetted out. He pointed at the wall, his mouth open in a silent laugh, clapped his hands, and stomped around, trying to find another trigger stone. With a loud "chunk" he found one a little further along the tunnel, only this time a volley of arrows came swishing out to clatter against the opposite wall, narrowly missing the capering pixie save for one that swept the hat right off his head.

"Professor!" Ginch lunged forward and grabbed him. "You okay?"

The Professor picked up his hat and put it back on, an arrow now sticking through it. He nodded.

Ginch gave him a hug and then shoved him. "Whatta you do, eh? Always you gotta play around." The Professor nodded and took out a paddleball and started smacking the little rubber ball in the air until Ginch slapped it from his hands. "No more! You gotta be careful!"

Sir Justinian walked past them and regarded the wall where the arrows had come out, looking impressed and pleased. "Now this is more what I was expecting. But why not start with—I know! The bubbles must be there to lull intruders into a false sense of security and then—thwock!—the arrows hit them completely by surprise. Ingenious!"

"Sure worked that way with the Professor, but I don't know . . . " Sir Justinian's theory made sense to Shade, but it just didn't feel right. It definitely wasn't the sort of thing that she had read in any book, and it seemed to her that that's how a book guardian would approach things—by the book. That was how she usually did things, after all.

The four continued more carefully than before. The tunnel rose and fell, twisted and turned, as they went deeper and deeper. As they walked, dust fell from the ceiling above, and pebbles sometimes tumbled from the wall to clatter in the gloom.

In time the tunnel opened up into a cavern, its ceiling so high that the light from their torches, lantern, and candle couldn't penetrate its darkness, but Shade could hear squeaks and a slight rustling of leathery wings from its depths. Milk-white stalagmites jutted up from the floor like jagged teeth in a giant mouth ready to chew up Shade and her friends. They wound their way through the jutting rocks and splashed through the puddles of the cavern until they came to a deep pit, stretching from wall to wall, at least fifty feet wide and fifty feet across. Sagging in the middle of it was a rickety bridge, its ropes fraying, its planks splintering. The four looked down but saw nothing but darkness.

"I wonder how deep it is and what's at the bottom," Shade said.

The Professor shrugged and dropped his candle. It stayed lit just long enough for them to catch a glimpse of a great mass of long, narrow, shiny, twisted shapes around thirty feet below. Shade thought she heard an annoyed hiss when the candle reached the bottom.

"Snakes?" Ginch shook his head and waved his hands. "Oh, no! I'm-a done. You go if you want but I'm-a go back because I no can-a deal with the slither and the hiss and the bite and . . . and . . . ugh! Fatcha-coota-matchca, snakes!"

Sir Justinian, meanwhile, had begun yanking at the posts, stakes, and ropes of the bridge. "Do not lose heart, Signore Ginch. The bridge, though old, seems sound."

"Hold on," Shade said and flew to the other side, taking care not to look down into the pit for she, while not as unnerved by snakes as Ginch, had no desire to look down and see a giant pit filled with them. She alighted on the other side and tested the posts and ropes. "They seem okay on this side too."

"There, you see? 'Tis perfectly safe, Signore Ginch."

"It's-a safe, eh?" Ginch frowned and looked at Sir Justinian. "Fine—you cross it."

"Excellent idea, good signore! If it can hold my weight, then we will know it's safe. Allow me to brave this Pit of Eternal Peril—"

"That's-a what we call it?" Ginch asked.

"Why are we naming it?" Shade called out. "And it's not 'eternal.' It only goes down about—"

"I shall brave the Pit of Eternal Peril," Sir Justinian continued, undaunted by his much less chivalrous companions who, unlike myself, seemed to have no appreciation for dramatic flair, "and be the first to face that which lies beyond!"

Shade gave a little wave. "Um, *hello*, I'm already on the other side."

"Watch and bear witness, my friends." Sir Justinian then, without hesitation or fear, heroically stepped onto the bridge. The planks creaked and cracked under his feet and strands of old brittle hemp strained and snapped as the ropes pulled taut under his weight, but the ancient bridge held. Sir Justinian slowly but confidently walked out to the middle of the bridge, one hand on the ropes, one hand holding his torch aloft. He turned around to face Ginch and the Professor. "See? 'Tis strong and sound as stone."

At that exact moment, Shade spotted movement high up. There, swinging down from the ceiling, was an immense and very sharp-looking blade. "Sir Justinian, look out!"

The good knight sprang back and narrowly missed being cut in two by the razor-sharp scythe that swung past. What was cut in two, however, was the bridge he stood on, plunging him into the pit.

Shade, without thinking, dived in to try to save her friend. It was a noble gesture but a foolish one, for his much greater weight would have dragged her down with him. But she wasn't fast enough and she watched in horror as her friend fell down, down, and disappeared in the snaky shadows below . . . and then watched in surprise as he came flying back up, arms and legs flailing, snakes sailing up all around him. She fluttered back just in time to avoid having Sir Justinian smash into her as he shot up past her. As he did, however, a shower of snakes rained up on Shade. She shrieked and swatted them off as Sir Justinian fell past her again, then shot back up again, this time laughing heartily as snakes again pelted Shade in his wake.

"'Tis some sort of soft and springy surface down below. Perfectly safe and, I must say, utterly delightful!" Sir Justinian declared as he bounded up out of the pit onto the far side next to Shade.

"Gah!" Shade cried as she slapped at snakes that bounced out of the pit with Sir Justinian and onto her. She stomped on the heads of the snakes on the ground until she finally realized that none of them were moving. She leaned down to examine one. After a couple of gentle pokes, Shade picked it up and looked at it carefully. "It's a fake. All of these snakes are fake."

"Come, my fairy friends, bounce across and join us here!" Sir Justinian shouted across the pit. "There is naught to fear unless you fear great amusement!"

Ginch looked down with dismay. "I no know . . .

Are you sure that—aah!" he cried as the Professor shoved him over the edge.

As Sir Justinian chuckled at Ginch's awkward bouncing and exceptionally rude comments about the Professor, Shade frowned at the remains of the rope bridge hanging down. *This makes no sense*, she thought. *If the bubbles were meant to lull us into a false sense of security so that we'd get killed by the arrows, then what's going on here? That blade could have killed Sir Justinian, so why make the pit harmless? And why make it possible to just bounce across?*

Ginch finally managed to bounce himself out of the pit and up next to her. "Fatcha-coota-matchca, pixie!" he shouted at the Professor, who jumped in and happily bounced up and down doing flips in the air. Ginch kicked a couple of fake snakes into the pit and reached up to grab one that was draped over his shoulder, then stopped. "'Ey, little Sprootshade. Do these snake-fakes gotta the fake tongues?"

"I didn't see any that did," Shade responded, still pondering the severed bridge.

"Uh-huh. And do these snake-fakes make-a the hiss?"

"No, how could they?" Shade asked, looking up.

"Then I no think they're all the snake-fakes," he said, panic in his eyes as he looked at the very real snake on his shoulders.

When their eyes met, the snake hissed and reared back, baring its fangs, ready to strike. Ginch gave a little whimper and closed his eyes just in time to not see Sir Justinian's hand whip out and snatch the snake off Ginch. "Why, I do believe this to be a Crom Cruach viper, one of the deadliest snakes in all Elfame! So that's Grigor's game here—get us to harmlessly play about until we're killed by these foul fiends. Cunning!"

"Maybe . . ." Shade said, not convinced but having no better explanation.

"Hey, partner! Up and out!" Ginch shouted at the Professor, who was tumbling merrily through the air. "The snake-fakes are no all fake!"

The Professor bounded back up, spun three somersaults in the air, and landed gracefully on the edge of the pit. He gave a little bow, then grabbed the three snakes that were hanging from his shoulders and sticking partially out of one pocket, at least one of which was real and wriggling, and shoved them into his pants.

"Should you really have a live, poisonous snake in your pocket?" Shade asked. The Professor shrugged. "I really don't think you should have poisonous creatures in your pockets." The Professor made a face and waved his hand dismissively.

Shade thought about trying to dissuade him more but decided to drop the matter—they had more pressing concerns and, she decided, what a pixie keeps in his pockets is his business and his alone, which I do believe is as close to words to live by as you, good Reader, are likely to find in this dreadful tome. And so they marched on into the darkness, unaware of what further perils might lurk there.

21

In which the peril becomes even
more perilous . . .

J ust past the pit, the cavern ended in a sheer rock
wall. At its base was an archway through which
a long straight passageway glowed with an eerie
blue light. Unlike the rough-hewn mining shafts that
they had passed through, this new tunnel was lined
with bricks and mortar. The blue light that filled the
tunnel, Shade quickly surmised, came from some sort
of phosphorescent lichen growing there.

At the end of the tunnel was a large square chamber whose ceiling glowed even more brightly with lichen, making their torches unnecessary. The chamber's granite walls were bare except the one on the far side, which was covered in elaborate bas-reliefs depicting great scenes from ancient fairy literature: King Quillwyrm pulling the butter knife from the enchanted stale loaf of rye bread, thus proving his right to rule; the mighty warrior Wolfbear beating the water troll with its own severed arm; St. Bartleby politely refusing to chase a questing beast; and many, many more. The room was empty save for a large, rectangular stone box in its center.

Shade and the others stepped cautiously into the room, scanning the ground for any trap triggers, and made their way to the sarcophagus. On its sides were carved scenes that told the history of the library of Alexandria: the building of the library, books being organized and shelved, people studying and reading, the library in flames, and finally a group of fairies running with books in their hands. The slab on top featured a crossed pickax and quill.

"I'll bet you anything that Grigor Byrrower's body and his book are in here," Shade said. She tried lifting the lid, but it wouldn't budge.

"Allow me, my good sprite," Sir Justinian said. He grasped the sides of the granite slab and with a mighty heave lifted the lid. Inside lay a figure dressed in ragged miner's pants, work shirt, and vest with a scarf tied over its head, its skin green and rough like tarnished copper. On its chest, clutched in the coblynau corpse's hands, lay a brown leather book.

"Okay, anybody else get-a the heebly-jeeblies from this?" Ginch asked. The Professor nodded in agreement. "I mean, we steal from everybody alla the time but we no steal from the dead body before."

"It's not stealing," Shade insisted, mostly convinced that she was right. "The plan was always for the members of G.L.U.G. to someday bring their books together, right? We're just doing what Grigor would want us to do."

"Yeah, because the arrows and the snakes and the blades that cut you in half, they all say 'Please come take-a the book'!"

"Grigor probably figured that anyone in G.L.U.G. would be smart enough to survive—and, guess what, he was right," Shade said. "I'm sure everything will be just fine."

She grabbed the book and pulled it free from the corpse's hands. Instantly, a stone slab crashed from the ceiling, blocking the chamber's only exit.

Ginch, the Professor, and Sir Justinian all looked at Shade. "Just-a fine, eh?"

"Okay, that way's blocked," Shade conceded. "But there's probably a secret way out, just like in more stories than I can think to name. We'll slowly and methodically search the room and—"

With a horrid scraping noise, the sarcophagus sank down until it stopped a couple of inches below the floor. The scraping sound, however, continued. It took Shade a moment to realize it was the walls on either side of the chamber, which were moving closer and closer.

The Professor whistled, pointed at the walls, pulled four pickled eggs out of his pocket, pointed to himself, Shade, Ginch, and Sir Justinian, then smushed the eggs between his hands. "The Professor says the walls, they're a-gonna squoosh us," Ginch explained.

"Stout hearts, chums!" Sir Justinian drew his sword. "I've fought my way out of tougher spots than this."

"And who you gonna fight?" Ginch asked. "I no think you can get-a the walls to make the surrender, paisan."

"Shut up a second and let me think!" Shade looked nervously from wall to wall. "I've read stories where walls close in like this. There's 'The Bronze Burial Blanket' by Mirecrossing . . . "

"How did the hero escape?" Sir Justinian asked hopefully as the walls inched closer and closer.

"He . . . uh . . . he got crushed to death." Shade frowned. "There's Edgar the Macabre's 'The Shaft and the Swinging Sword.'"

"And how did-a that one end?"

"Somebody came and pulled the guy out at the last minute."

"Excellent!" Sir Justinian cried. "I shall go out and then break in and save you all just in the nick of time."

"And how you gonna get outta the room to get back inna the room to get us out?"

Sir Justinian's smile faded. "Well . . . "

"Let me think. In one book, they—that's it! The wall carvings! One of them has to trigger a secret door!"

"That's-a great! So which one do we push?"

Shade considered her options. "I'm not sure. Let me think—"

"We no gotta the time to think. We gotta the time to either get squooshed or no get squooshed. Personally, I prefer to no get squooshed."

"There's always time to think things through."

"Not now there isn't, fatcha-coota-matchca, sproot!"

As the two fairies bickered, Sir Justinian reached out and strained to hold back the walls, but even his great might was no match for the inevitable crush of the death trap. The Professor looked back and forth and back and forth from one wall to the other, faster and faster, until he staggered and nearly fell from dizziness. As he looked down, he whistled and pointed at the sarcophagus lid.

"Good idea, my pixie compatriot!" Sir Justinian grabbed the slab and, muscles bulging and tendons straining from the effort, mightily hoisted high the slab. The walls ground closer, ever closer, until they rested on either side of the lid. The scraping of stone against stone stopped. All was quiet in the tomb.

"Great work, Sir Justinian!" Shade smirked at Ginch. "See. No reason to panic—there *is* time to think things through."

Suddenly a loud crack sounded and fissures formed all over the slab's surface.

"Okay, that's-a the reason to panic!" Ginch and the Professor shoved Shade back and began slapping and yanking at the wall carvings with wild abandon as the slab continued to crack, their efforts becoming more and more frenzied as more and more of the coffin lid crumbled. Then the slab finally gave, breaking in the middle and falling with a crash to the floor. The fairies' efforts reached a fever pitch, their arms blurs of motion. Then, just as all seemed lost, the Professor, springing high, grabbed hold of the carving of King

Quillwyrm's butter knife, which flipped down. There was a click and the wall swung back to reveal a pitch-black tunnel. The three fairies and Sir Justinian dove into the darkness in time to watch the walls grind the remains of the sarcophagus lid into powder and extinguish the torches they had left behind in the chamber, plunging them into darkness.

"See?" Ginch panted. "If you no think there's-a the reason to panic, then you've never done-a the panic right. Now we need some light."

Just then, as if written by some ham-fisted hack writer, a tiny, faraway light appeared, and they began to hear a low growl and panting. As they watched, the light got closer and closer, and the growling and panting got louder and louder. They couldn't make out what it was, but it didn't sound the least bit friendly.

"You know, now that I think on it, maybe we no need some light," Ginch whispered.

22

In which exciting investment opportunities arise . . .

The light got brighter and brighter, almost blinding, and behind it Shade saw what looked like arms waving—some pointed, some pincered, some rounded—and two thick, wide-set legs underneath that, oddly enough, didn't seem to move even though the beast was getting closer. Its growl grew and its breathing came out in a regular, rhythmic "chuff-chuff-chuff."

"Behind me, friends!" Sir Justinian shouted over the creature's cacophony as he drew his sword. "I shall vanquish this dread beast—"

"'Ey, look!" Ginch shouted. "There's-a the little guy riding piggledyback."

"I shall vanquish this dread beast and its dastardly master or die trying! Yaaaah!" Sir Justinian raised high his blade and charged into the light.

"Wait!" Shade cried. "I'm not sure that that's—"

Over the growls and pants Shade heard the clang and crash of metal striking metal, then a smash and the light went out. There were more clangs and shouts from Sir Justinian in the darkness. The growls abruptly ceased and the pants slowly died. "Ha-ha! I have killed the beast!"

"You dented my Automole and smashed its head-lamp!" someone shouted. A match flared in the darkness and then a lantern sprang to light. There in front of Shade was something like a small tank with an array of metal arms fitted with tongs, drills, circular saw blades, pickaxes, and shovels mounted on the top. Sitting in the middle surrounded by levers and buttons was a coblynau, a scarf tied around the top of his head on top of which was perched a pair of goggles. A lean, muscular arm, its skin having the color and sheen of polished copper, lifted the lantern up higher, and Shade could see shock and outrage on the mining fairy's shiny face. "Why would you do that?"

Sir Justinian looked confused. "Because it appeared to be a foul, bloodthirsty beast that—"

"Oh, you do NOT call my baby a foul anything!" The coblynau pointed an accusatory finger at the knight as he stroked the dashboard of his vehicle with his other hand as if to comfort it. "What are you doing in my tunnels?"

"Your tunnels?" Shade put her hands on her hips. "Really? Because we happen to know that these are the tunnels of Grigor Byrrower."

"No, they *were* Great-Uncle Grigor's tunnels. Then they were my dad's. Now they're mine. Oh, ha! Pun! Didn't even mean to make one. Because, you know, like, 'mine' and 'mine.'"

"Oh. Then . . . I guess we're looking for you?"

"Really?" The coblynau looked puzzled, and then his face lit up with excitement. "Are you investors?"

"Investors?" Shade echoed.

"You should have said something! But maybe you wanted to, like, do a sneak inspection of the place before getting a more official tour to make sure everything is on the up-and-up. Very shrewd on your part! Very shrewd," the cobynau gushed, his voice rising and falling in a singsongy manner.

"We're-a no—"

"Not gonna lie to you, but you couldn't have picked a worse place to start!" the coblynau continued, completely oblivious to Ginch's attempt to speak. "I'm, like, barely a quarter of the way through this attraction. I'm thinking of calling it 'The Curse of the Coblynau's Crypt,' but I haven't decided yet. What I can tell you is that Great-Uncle Grigor designed this place to be an *actual* deathtrap-filled tomb. Can you believe that? I mean, like, who does that? So I'm replacing all the real traps with fake ones. You know, like, bubble jets instead of arrows, a bounce pit with fake snakes instead of a real pit filled with spikes and vipers, and such. You're lucky you weren't, like, killed in there."

"We almost were!" Shade replied.

"To be honest, I'm not done with this one. That's why I put up the 'Danger! Keep Out!' sign . . . but now that I think of it, that does kind of fit the theming I'm going with on this attraction, so, like, that's kind of my fault, I guess. Anyway, if you're looking to invest, what you really need to look at—"

"Whoa, whoa, whoa!" Shade held up her hands to quiet the enthusiastic coblynau. "Can we talk about all of this someplace a little less . . . deathtrap-y?"

"Of course! Tell you what, climb up on the Automole—"

"The Otto-what?" Ginch asked.

"Mole, mole," the coblynau said.

The Professor lifted up his shirt and pointed to a small brown bump on his belly.

"Ha! Wrong kind of mole, but tidy pun that is!" the coblynau laughed, which earned a thumbs-up from the Professor. "It's an all-purpose mining vehicle I invented. It's got, like, a chamber of salamanders that, when excited, flame up and boil a tankful of water, which then produces steam that moves pistons that—but I'm probably boring all of you with all this technical mumbo jumbo, aren't I?"

"Yeah," Ginch stated bluntly. The Professor nodded.

"'Tis a bit hard to follow, I must say, my good mining fairy."

"It's Elidyr. Elidyr Byrrower."

"No doubt, good mining fairy. No doubt."

Shade cleared her throat to get Elidyr's attention back. "So, are we going . . . or . . . "

"Oh, yeah, yeah, yeah! Like I was saying, hop on and I'll give you a ride out of these tunnels. The Automole's kind of loud, so how about we go back to my cabin and talk there? It's not far."

Not waiting for an answer, the coblynau pulled a couple of levers and flipped a switch and the Automole roared and chugged once more. Shade and her friends scrambled on and rode up and up until finally they emerged from the mines and into the early afternoon. Elidyr parked the Automole next to a pony cart. Between the two was a metal pole from the top of which extended a long bar. Elidyr reached up, grasped the bar, then swung himself out of the Automole cockpit and over to the driver's seat of the cart. When he did so, Shade saw that his legs were strapped together.

"Did you have an accident or something?" Shade asked.

Elidyr looked puzzled for a moment. "Oh, my legs? No. They haven't worked since I was born."

Shade, having been a relatively sheltered fairy, had never seen a fairy like this. Sure, she had known sprites who had gotten too old to fly and fairies who walked with a limp and had to use a cane to get around, but never one that couldn't walk at all. "I'm sorry," she said.

Elidyr shrugged. "For what? I get along just fine. To be honest, I feel sorry for you. Because I have to work harder and be smarter to do all the stuff that comes easy to you, I'm inventing things like my Automole and coming up with ideas like my amusement center."

"I'm sorry, good mining fairy, but you keep talking of things like 'attractions' and 'amusement centers' but I know not of what you speak," Sir Justinian said.

"Yeah, you talk-a the nonsense," Ginch agreed.

"It's not nonsense—it's a great opportunity for the people who live around here and for investors like you. I've taken the money my family has made in mining and, like, hired some of the out-of-work miners to turn these hills into a place for people to have fun."

"So you build-a the tavern," Ginch said. The Professor gave a thumbs up, pulled a mug of mead from his coat, saluted Elidyr, and gulped it down.

"No. This isn't going to be some minging old pub. This is going to be a place that fairies will come from all over Elfame to see."

"So it's-a gonna be the big, fancy tavern," Ginch replied. The Professor took out, toasted with, and drained another mug of mead, then burped.

"*It's not a tavern!* It's going to be, like, a place where

entire families can have a good time and *don't you dare say it's a tavern again*," Elidyr said as Ginch opened his mouth and the Professor took out another drink. "It'll have rides that show you the beauty of the underground world or, like, whip you through tunnels at an alarming rate but safely so it'll be terrifying and fun at the same time, and we'll take an old mining camp and rebuild it with lush mining-themed restaurants and gift shops, and I was thinking that maybe we'd create some cute and lovable characters, like maybe Gary the Gold Nugget or Bituminous Betty, and a cantankerous old miner with—"

"Actually, before you go on too much more, I should tell you we're not potential investors," Shade admitted.

Elidyr looked surprised. "Then who are you and why were you in my mines?"

"Well, I'm a junior librarian, he's a knight errant, and those two are crooks," Shade explained.

"We prefer 'fairies of fortune,'" Ginch said. He and the Professor tipped their hats to Elidyr.

"They're crooks. And we came to the Hollow Hills

for this." Shade took the book they'd taken from Grigor Byrrower's hands from her backpack.

"Why would you come for a prop from my attraction?" Elidyr asked.

"Well, I'll have you know that what you have here is a lot more than just some prop," Shade explained. "In fact, this . . . " Shade trailed off as she flipped from blank page to blank page. "What the donkle is this?"

Elidyr's face lit up. "Oh, I get it! You're, like, one of those Garglers, aren't you?"

"That's-a 'Gloogers,'" Ginch said.

"No, it's *G.L.U.G.ers*." Shade frowned, irritated.

"And you thought that was my great-uncle's codebook. Sorry, but it seemed dumb to keep a good book hidden in some musty crypt, so when I took over the mines from my parents, I put the codebook in my cabin. That's just, like, an empty journal I put there to keep the compression chamber from going off and, you know, to make it look good."

Shade punched Ginch hard in the arm. "Ow! 'Ey, whatta you do, fatcha-coota-matchca, sproot?"

"I don't know him well enough to punch him."

"All right, that's-a fair," Ginch said, rubbing his shoulder.

"Here, since I was, like, going to take you to my cabin anyway, we'll go there and get you that book," Elidyr said agreeably.

"Okay, but first we should go and get our mule and cart," Shade said.

"That's unicorn," said a gravelly voice from the trees surrounding the tunnel entrance. "And I wouldn't go back for the cart if I were you. Unless you really wanna be captured, killed, and maybe eaten."

23

In which an offer is declined, and
the seeds of doubt are sown . . .

"What are you talking about?" Shade demanded.

"You have a talking mule?" Elidyr
asked. "That's tidy, that is!"

"I'm actually a unicorn. And this gang of red caps
just showed up—a couple goblins, a spriggan, a wulver—talking about lying in wait to ambush you and
take 'the little bug girl' back to their boss. Then that

spriggan complained about being hungry and started looking at me and getting all drooly, so I bolted."

Shade frowned. "The goblins. Did they have hyena heads?"

Trudgemore nodded. "Yeah. Couldn't tell the difference between 'em. Sorry if that sounds fairiest of me but—."

"Wait here, everyone." Shade flew up and around the side of the grassy hill. When she made it to the other side, she spied the waterfall and the pool outside the cave entrance and there, waiting with clubs and swords in hand, were the goblin twins, Laffer and Gaffer, Wolfgang the wulver, and the spriggan Struggs. The same gang that Shade and her friends had fought when she first made her way to the Grand Library. The same gang employed by the Sluagh noblewoman who had sworn vengeance on Shade: Lady Perchta, the Duchess of Sighs.

So it is *Perchta who's been hunting the members of G.L.U.G.*, Shade thought as she fluttered back to the others. *I knew it! She must want the books so that she and the Sluagh Horde can attack and defeat the Seelie Court. There must be something really, really powerful in those books.*

Shade and the others hurried off to Elidyr's cabin. Perched atop the next hill over, it was a cozy, one-story affair made of golden-brown logs topped with a grass-covered roof on which three small goats were grazing. "Helps keep the house cool in summer and warm in winter," Elidyr explained as he pulled up to a post and bar similar to the one on the hillside and swung himself down from the cart and into a wheeled chair. "Come on inside and we'll get that book."

The first thing that Shade noticed about the cabin when they got inside was that the shelves holding books and blankets and other odds and ends were all mounted fairly low on the walls. The second thing she noticed was that there were so many books. Scanning the shelf nearest to her, she saw books of poetry: *The Collected Works of Belle of Amherst*, Whitman's *Blades of Barley*, Letterrate and Charhill's *Lyrical Ballads*, and many others.

"That's, like, the poetry section. I've got the books arranged by content. And right here, in the adventure section, is the book you're looking for." Elidyr pulled out *An Expedition to the Underground World* by Verne de Feydeau and handed it to Shade. "Great-Uncle Grigor's copy of the secret message is tucked inside."

Shade hugged the book to her chest. "This is wonderful! We've got all the codebooks now. The others are waiting at the Grand Library. We can all go back there, decode the message, and get the books!"

Elidyr looked embarrassed. "That sounds great, but to be honest, like . . . I'm not coming along."

"What?" Shade was shocked. Then, looking at Elidyr's chair, she thought she understood. "Oh, no, don't worry—the Grand Library doesn't have any stairs. It's one big ramp, so your chair would totally—"

"It's not that," Elidyr explained. "I've been to the library a few times and it's great. And even if it didn't have the ramp, I'd, like, figure out a way to make it work."

"Then why—"

"What it is is I've got too much to do here. My dream is to build something great, something *new*, something Elfame's never seen before. And we're getting close to being done. I can't leave that right now."

"But what about your great-uncle's dream of bringing those books back to the world?" Shade asked.

Elidyr smiled. "It's a good dream, and I'm really glad that you and other people are going to, like, make it come true and that I was able to help, but it's not *my* dream, no matter how much Great-Uncle Grigor and my parents tried to make it be. They lived their lives. I have to live mine."

As Elidyr gave them all a ride back to the library tree, Shade pondered what Elidyr had said. *All I've ever wanted to do was live around books, and this is taking me away from them and putting my life and the lives of my friends at risk. And for what? To find a few books? Is that really worth it? And am I doing this because it's what*

Dad would have wanted or because it's what I *want?*
Shouldn't I know?

When they arrived at the Grand Library, Shade had no answers as they went in to decipher a code that had gone unbroken for more than a hundred years.

24

In which the location of the lost
books is revealed . . .

"The Grand Scrutinizer has yet to return," Johannes informed Shade as most of the library staff, Poor Richard, the Bowser twins, Sir Justinian, Grouse, and even Trudgemore (whose ability to talk and read settled all objections to the presence of a pack mule/alleged unicorn in the Grand Library) gathered in one of the library's private meeting rooms late that afternoon.

"But I'm sure he will," Émilie said grimly.

"What about the books on the list I gave you?" Shade asked.

"Interest dropped a bit later in the day, but still they vere looked at."

On a large table, Shade and the other members of G.L.U.G. spread out four identical code sheets and the five codebooks. "Okay," Shade said. "Everybody, grab your books and decode your code sheets."

Ginnie and Ronnie Bowser both grabbed *The Fairy Godfather* and tugged it back and forth. "Shoove off, Gin," Ronnie said, attempting to yank the book. "This is me book."

"Like fun it is," Ginnie replied as she jerked the book free. "Gran would want *me* to have it!"

Ronnie made a grab for the book. "Don't yez bring Gran into this, Gin!"

Shade rolled her eyes and slid Martinko's book across the table to them. "Here, blueberry-brains. One of you can go through that."

Glaring at her sister, Ronnie picked up Martinko's

book and everyone started flipping through pages and jotting down words. When they were done, they all slid their papers to Shade who tried combination after combination of words. She eventually stopped. *"On the north face of Mount Wyrd, high in the ruined Tower of Dead Souls,"* she read aloud. "Sounds kind of creepy."

The others looked at her in disbelief. "Do you . . . understand what you just read?" Émilie asked delicately.

"Yeah. We're going to have to climb the biggest dingle-dangle mountain in Elfame, which is going to be a real pain, to get to some run-down tower—"

"You no know about the Tower of the Dead Souls?" Ginch asked.

Shade's face grew hot with embarrassment. She hated having to admit when she didn't know something. "No, but—"

"Surely, Lady Shade, you have heard tales of the dreaded Robin Redcap," Sir Justinian said.

"Well . . . maybe one or two . . . "

"That's-a the bluff! I know the bluff when I see it, and that's-a the bluff," Ginch declared. "How can you no know about the Robin Redcap?"

"Maybe because I grew up in the middle of nowhere! So who the donkle is Robin Redcap?"

"Robin Redcap is the most feared fairy of all time," Johannes explained.

"Zey say zat 'e is zousands of seasons old and feasts upon ze blood and ze souls of fairies," François said.

"Murders 'em with the sickle he always carries," Ronnie said.

"Don't forget how he dyes his hat red with the blood of his victims, Ronnie," Ginnie added.

"I'm not forgetting that, Gin! I were joost pausin' for dramatic effect, which yez joost ruined."

"That's-a why the Sluagh goons wear the red caps," Ginch explained. "They think it make them look tough and scary, like the Robin Redcap."

The Professor whistled and pointed at his foot.

"I was-a gettin' to the iron shoes! Robin Redcap wears the iron shoes."

"He's the only fairy unharmed by cold iron," Sir Justinian said, squinting and stroking his chin.

Grouse's shoulders slumped. "Oh, no . . . He's going to say it's—"

"A worthy challenge!" Sir Justinian smiled broadly. Grouse groaned and buried his face in his hands. "My loyal squire, Grouse, and I will gladly join you."

Poor Richard sighed. "I'm afraid my frailty must keep me here. Perhaps it's just as well—poor Martinko's life still hangs in the balance."

"Well, I'm as strong as an ox," Ronnie Bowser declared.

"And twice as ugly," Ginnie said.

"Only 'cause I look like yez," Ronnie shot back. "I'm coomin'."

"That goes double for me," Ginnie said. "My sister and I are going to make Gran proud."

Everyone looked expectantly at Shade. *They're all counting on me*, Shade fretted. She turned to her friends, who had been with her ever since she left Pleasant Hollow. If they said no, would she have the courage to go on without them? Would their refusal be enough justification for remaining behind herself? "Ginch? Professor? What about you?"

The two uneasily tugged at their shirt collars. "Wait a minote. We gotta consider the pros and the cons and make the informed decision." The two turned their backs to the others and huddled together. Both gestured animatedly while Ginch whispered. After a few moments they straightened up, and Ginch flipped a gold coin in the air, caught it, and slapped it down on the back of his hand. He slowly peeked at it and frowned. "Heads. Fatcha-coota-matchca, coin! Looks like we go with you."

That's it, then, I suppose, Shade thought. "Okay. We leave tomorrow morning."

"But why wait? Adventure calls now!" Sir Justinian unsheathed his sword and pointed it up at the ceiling.

"It'd be really nice if Adventure would shut its stupid face for once," Grouse grumbled.

"One: It'll be night soon, and I don't think we want to be scaling a mountain at night," Shade explained.

"Two: We'll need to gather food and other supplies. Three: It would probably be good for at least one of us to read up on mountain climbing. Four: I think Lady Perchta is the one who's been trying to kill all the G.L.U.G.ers and beat us to the lost books, so—"

"Perchta?" Sir Justinian's eyes narrowed. "You're sure?"

"Almost positive," Shade said. "The fairies who were going to ambush us were some of the ones we fought when she attacked us on the Marble Cliffs six months ago."

"Then we no gotta worry about the Perchta, eh?" Ginch said, sounding a little relieved. "She must be back in the Hollow Hills."

"I don't know. Think about it—over the past few days, we've been attacked in some way, shape, or form in Cottinghamtownshireborough, Bilgewater, and the Hollow Hills. There's no way anyone can get to all of those places that fast."

The Professor cleared his throat and pointed at himself, Ginch, and Shade.

"Okay, sure, *we* did, but only because the Grand

Library is in all of those places—again, *how* I'm still not sure of." The Professor pulled a slate and piece of chalk out and began to scribble mathematical equations. "Not now, Professor. Anyway, she must have troops or agents everywhere that she sends orders to, using—I don't know—birds or magic mirrors or something. So *she* could be anywhere, and so could goons working for her."

"But this Perchta, she wouldn't know about Mount Wyrd, would she?" Ginnie said. "After all, we just found out ourselves."

"For once, me sis's right aboot soomethin'," Ronnie agreed. "No need to worry."

They've got a point, Shade thought, but she had an uneasy feeling. "We still need to prepare."

"Oh, I shall prepare," Sir Justinian said. "The chance to square off against both a nigh-invulnerable creature and my most hated foe? Fortune surely smiles."

"I just want to eat an entire cheesecake and die." Grouse sighed. The Professor reached into his coat and pulled out a cheesecake. "That's covered in lint," Grouse said.

The Professor shrugged, pulled out a fork, and began eating.

•

A knock on her door roused Shade in her small reading chair where she was surrounded by books. "Dozed off studying?" Poor Richard asked from the doorway.

"Yeah." Shade yawned and stretched. "I was just trying to get ready for tomorrow."

"Often, studying too much can leave one just as unready as not enough," the cowlug said, leaning on his cane. "And what have you managed to learn?"

"Not a lot. What little there is on Robin Redcap and the Tower of Dead Souls seems pretty dodgy. Other than that, I think I've got the basics of mountain climbing down, all of which seems to amount to 'don't fall.'" Shade sighed. "I wish we could be better prepared than that, but I guess it'll have to do."

"I get the sense that your reluctance to sally forth isn't just about a lack of preparation, is it?"

Shade wanted to object, but Richard's kind, knowing eyes stopped her. "I . . . I don't know why I'm doing all this. Or if I *should* be doing this. I mean, I should know, right? What we're doing could get me *killed*. Could get my friends *killed*. For what? Because my dad wanted me to do it because his dad wanted him to do it and his dad and the rest of you before him? Maybe Elidyr had the right idea. Maybe I should just abandon this stupid quest and stay in the library where I belong. No offense—I know that you've lived your whole life for this and—"

"Oh, pish tosh! I haven't lived my life just to find those books. I've experimented and written and disputed and had the time of my life all these years. As for doing this for me or Alexandria or your great-grandfather—or for your father for that matter—well . . . Do you know what my father, Richard Freeholder the III, did for a living?"

"No."

"He was one of the wealthiest landowners in our little corner of Elfame. Collected the rents and lorded it over the common folk. 'Rich by name, rich by nature,' they used to say of him, and he wanted me to be just like him when I grew up."

"And what did you do?" Shade asked.

"I ran away and hid in a library," Richard chuckled. "And when I inherited my father's lands, I sold them off and happily squandered my wealth on science and learning and charity."

"But isn't finding these books a lot more important than just, I don't know, making money and being snooty?"

"I most certainly would agree with that, but not everyone would. One man's mountain is another man's molehill and vice versa. But to get to the heart of the matter, once upon a time, a small group of book lovers did what we thought was best. What matters now is that *you* do the same, regardless of what any of us have ever wanted."

Shade nodded. "Thanks. That helps. I think."

"I hope it does. Well, I'm off to tinker a bit on my latest project and do more poison research. I believe I'm on the verge of a breakthrough on both fronts." Poor Richard began to walk away, then stopped. "Do you know what your great-grandfather Moonshadow would probably say about you going tomorrow just for his sake?"

"No. What?"

"I believe he'd say, 'Get donkled!' Heh, heh! Such language he used! I do wonder if he kissed his mother with that mouth . . . " Chuckling as he went, Poor Richard left Shade to her thoughts.

Well, I guess I'm off the hook if I want to be, Shade thought. *But is that what I want?*

She lay on her bed, hoping both sleep and an answer to her dilemma would come quickly. Neither did.

25

In which not enough breakfast is

eaten . . .

E ven though she was famished, Shade didn't go straight to the staff dining hall when she awoke the next morning. Instead, she walked down the spiral ramp and ran her hands along the books filling the shelves. *I know what my dad would want me to do,* she thought, *but I still don't know what I really want to do. I think I want to go, but I need to know why.*

Just as she thought this, she came to one of the many areas formed in the branches that grew out from the great library tree's trunk. But this was not just any area: It was the new children's section. "They sure got this done in a hurry," Shade muttered, impressed. Colorful books filled the low shelves running the length of the room. Picture windows with padded window seats filled the walls, each window looking out on a different part of Elfame: rolling hills and stretching plains, bustling towns and sleepy villages, roaring seas and babbling brooks. There were tables for art, chairs and sofas for reading, and there at the far end was a slightly raised stage with a big chair sur-rounded by large, floofy pillows. Shade smiled. *I wish I had someplace like when I was little*, she mused.

Shade scanned the shelves until she found a thin red book: *Goodnight, Little Sprite*, her favorite book from childhood. She paged through it and thought about how her own copy was lost when her home burned and how she had feared the story had been lost forever.

But the story wasn't gone. It was there in the Grand Library and always would be, safe and sound and waiting for her, for *any* reader who came looking for it. And then she knew why.

Shade put the book back and marched off to the dining hall. She threw open the doors and put her hands on her hips. "All right, everyone. We're going to climb Mount Wyrd and get those books because books aren't meant to be locked up or hidden or buried in private collections. They're meant to be read and read by everyone and, donkle it all, they belong in *libraries* where that can happen, so we are going to go up that mountain and bring the lost books of Alexandria home!"

Everyone at the table sat frozen mid-bite. "Can we finish the breakfast first?" Ginch asked sheepishly as the Professor slid some slices of toast into his pocket and then spooned in some jam.

"Yes," Shade declared resolutely. "Because I am hungry."

"I wish I had eaten more at breakfast," Shade grumbled hours later as she, Ginch, the Professor, Sir Justinian, and Ginnie Bowser scaled the black rock cliffs of Mount Wyrd while far below the turbulent northern sea roared up at the iron-gray sky. Following the mountain climbing guidelines Shade had read, her companions were tied to each other by rope with Sir Justinian, the biggest and strongest of them, at the top. Shade, however, was not tied to them. Instead, she took the lead, her reasoning being that, should she fall, she could fly herself to safety. Down below, Grouse and Trudgemore reluctantly stood guard by the library tree while Ronnie Bowser, at her insistence, went back to Bilgewater to get reinforcements—or, as she said, "try again to find the lads and round oop any other geezers what weren't copped by the bizzies," in case Lady Perchta managed to track them all down.

There was a lull in the wind, so Shade fluttered up the mountainside a bit to look for especially treacherous stretches or flat places where they could stop for a rest. To her relief, she found a grassy plateau where evergreens grew near a pool of water. She flew down to let the others know, then returned to the plateau to give her aching muscles a rest.

Shade shirked off her backpack and splashed water on her face to wash off the sweat. As the water dripped from her chin, she heard a scuttling noise.

"Well, I, for one, am famished. What do you sssupose there'll be?" a voice whispered.

"Sssomething tasssty, no doubt," another replied.

Shade wiped her eyes and looked around to see who had spoken, but she saw no one. Then she looked up.

There, crawling along the face of the cliff were two figures with extremely long arms and legs that appeared to have an extra set of joints, making their already bizarre movements even more alien and unnerving. Their black hair and robes blended in so perfectly with the black stone of the mountain that Shade might have missed them completely if not for their bare, purplish-red hands and feet—if indeed, they can be called their feet since they looked exactly like their hands, with the fingers being extra long and thin and, like their legs, featuring an extra joint. Shade yelped in surprise. The two creatures turned, revealing the faces of beautiful women. Beautiful, that is, if you find eight black spider-like eyes beautiful (you know, like your cousin D'Artagnan does, bless his creepy soul!).

Shade froze, unsure whether she would be considered "sssomthing tasssty," and unsure how much she could do about it if she were. The wall-crawlers—which, with your exceptionally impressive knowledge of fairies, I'm sure I don't need to note were gwyllion—also froze. Three sets of eyes (eighteen eyes total) stared at one another in silence. Shade slowly raised one of her hands and gave a slight wave. "Uh . . . hi?"

Each gwyll slowly raised a hand, to return the wave or to attack, Shade wasn't sure, for at that exact moment Sir Justinian ran forward, sword in hand, shielding Shade's body behind his own. "If thou seekest a snack, then prepare thyself for a bellyful of cold steel!"

The gwyllion shrieked and skittered away around the

corner of the cliffside. Sir Justinian scanned the area. "We seem to be safe for now, my friends, but be on your guard. Danger doubtlessly stalks the mountain—"

"I'm not sure they were dangerous," Shade interjected.

"—and spies for the vile villain we seek to vanquish no doubt lurk around every corner."

"'Ey, nobody said the nothing about vansquishing nobody." Ginch flopped on the ground as the Professor slurped from the pool. "I thought we just get-a the books."

Ginnie Bowser swatted dust from her fur coat. "I've never backed down from a fight in my life—when you're a fake gangster, it's considered very poor form— but if we can sneak in and get the books without a fight, I think that would be for the best."

"Agree to disagree. Wait here while I secure the area." The knight slowly made his way around the edge of the clearing and back behind some trees.

Ginnie nodded after him. "Does he ever ease up?"

"No," they all replied just as Sir Justinian shouted, "Ha-ha! Come, my friends, come!"

With a chorus of groans, Shade and the others reluctantly followed his voice to a gap between two large boulders. On the other side, rough steps were hewn into the rock, leading high up the mountainside and vanishing in the mists above.

"Follow me." Sir Justinian bounded up the stairs. "Adventure awaits!"

"I'm-a gonna take my time," Ginch grumbled. "Adventure, I no think she's inna the rush."

So the crew climbed the stairs with Sir Justinian in the lead, dashing up to see what was ahead and then doubling back again and again to his pokey compatriots to urge them on in much the same way your spaniel, Captain Wilberforce, does when you try to have a nice leisurely walk in the woods. But, because these are quite dreadful fairies (as I have noted on various occasions), the knight's exhortations did in no way stir deep wells of nobility or inspire heroic enthusiasm. Thus, they trudged slowly upward.

After a solid hour of climbing, the Professor came to an abrupt halt. "What are you—?" Shade began to ask but stopped when the Professor held his finger to his lips.

The four fairies stood still and listened. From the stairs below they heard a clack, clack, clack, like stones tapping against each other. The clacking grew louder and closer. As Shade watched, it looked like four little gold nuggets floated up and around a corner of the black stairway, but as the nuggets drew a little closer, Shade could see they were eyes, eyes belonging to two fairies about half her size, their rounded bodies translucent and smooth like polished quartz.

"Just because I hev not finished does not mean I hev nothing to contribute, käraste," one said with a shrug.

"A week you hed, Steinn. A week!"

"Still no sign of the beast," Sir Justinian announced as he came pounding down the steps. His eyes grew wide as he spied the quartz fairies, whose shiny gold eyes also widened as he pointed his sword at them. "More agents of Robin Redcap, no doubt hoping to ambush us from behind!"

The two quartz fairies yelped and curled themselves

up into little crystal balls that clattered swiftly down the steps.

"I return at an opportune time," Justinian said. "A moment later, and those dastardly devils might very well have waylaid thee."

"'Ey, I see them coming," Ginch objected.

Ginnie Bowser cracked her knuckles. "And I can handle myself just fine."

"Um, they didn't look like they were going to be any trouble," Shade said.

Sir Justinian slapped her hard on the back. "That's the spirit! I'm glad to hear that some of your mother's warrior mettle is buried there under your ample book-ish softness."

Shade frowned. "Okay, first, *rude*. Second, what I meant was that I don't think they were going to—"

"Come, friends—we shall remain together from here on out, lest danger, which dogs our heels, bite us when we are unawares."

"I really don't think those two were after us," Shade muttered.

"Let us press on to the Tower of Dead Souls!" The knight declared with a flourish of his sword.

"Can we no say the name no more?" Ginch grumbled as they all followed. "It make-a my stomach hurt."

As the sun climbed higher and higher, the black rock of Mount Wyrd began to redden, first into burgundy and then maroon. Finally, when the sun reached its noontime peak, it blazed crimson, the color of fresh blood, as do all of the Fola Dubh Mountains at high noon. Ginch looked around nervously. "You know, I think we got plenty of the books already. How's about we—"

"Shh!" Sir Justinian whispered down to him. "The end of our quest is nigh. Come."

The fairies crept up the stairs behind Sir Justinian. Just as he had said, the stairs finally came to an end in front of a gap in a crumbling stone wall. On the other side was a well-tended garden divided into boxed beds filled with herbs and flowers and vegetables with blossoming fruit trees growing on its edges. At the far end a tall ivy-covered stone tower stood, but just barely, for it leaned dangerously. Large stones that had fallen from its sides littered the ground.

And there, standing at its entrance, was a tall, powerfully built, and hideously ugly fairy. Leathery skinned, thickly muscled arms and legs showed through the holes in his ragged clothing. Pebbles ground noisily under his iron boots. In his hand, he held a sickle, its half-moon blade shining in the sun. And on his head, perched above bulging, bloodshot eyes, beaky nose, and wide, thin-lipped mouth, was a red cap, wet and dripping with what looked like fresh blood.

26

In which there *should* be an epic
battle with an evil beast, but . . .

S hade, Ginch, the Professor, and Ginnie Bowser
dove behind the wall. When Sir Justinian didn't
budge, grim determination on his face, Shade
tugged his arm until he joined them out of sight of the
creature. "My fairy friends, it ill befits a knight of the
realm to cower in the face of terror."

"We're not cowering," Shade said.

"Speak for yourself," Ginch said. "I'm a-cowerin'."

The Professor pointed to himself and Ginnie and nodded. "I'm . . . strategizing, not cowering," Ginnie explained lamely.

"Look, we don't know what exactly we're dealing with here," Shade whispered to the overeager knight as they all peered into the garden. "Before we go charging in, we need to figure out the best course of action. For example, what if—"

Suddenly a chilly gray mist swirled past her. It flowed over to the fearsome fairy, then condensed to form a ghastly, gaunt woman in an emerald green dress and gray cloak. Flaming red hair hung down to her waist, framing her pale face and green, bloodshot, weeping eyes. In her hands she clutched a long white sheet, which she held out toward the red-capped fairy.

"A banshee!" Sir Justinian gasped. "And with a burial shroud for the beast!"

"That looks more like a tablecloth," Shade said.

"Verily, 'tis a shroud!"

"But look—on the edge it's all lacy and—"

"She has clearly come to shriek the soul of Robin Redcap to beyond the veil." Sir Justinian, eyes flashing, drew his sword and charged into the garden. "Have at thee, Robin Redcap!"

The brutal-looking fairy slumped and gave an annoyed sigh. "Really? Fiona, get back while I take care of this. Look, the name's Cuthbert. Robin was my—hey!" The fairy blocked Sir Justinian's down-sweeping sword with his sickle and sent him staggering back with a metal-shoed kick to the chest. "Would you knock it off, please? I'm really sick of—"

But Cuthbert was unable to finish because Sir Justinian lashed out, the pommel of his sword connecting with the fairy's nose. There was a sickening crunch, and the fairy dropped his sickle and put his hands to his face. "I thing you broge my nose, you creeb!" he said.

"I'll break more than that, foul fiend!" Sir Justinian swung at Cuthbert, but the red cap punched him in the side, grabbed and lifted him in the air, then slammed him to the ground. Sir Justinian gawped and struggled to catch his breath.

Cuthbert grabbed his now crooked nose and jerked it back in place with a snap. "Ow! Fiona, hide in the tower! This one's dangerous!" He raised his foot high above Sir Justinian's head.

"Wait!" Shade dashed toward the two brawlers.

Sir Justinian's hands shot up and grabbed the iron boot. "I *am* dangerous, villain," he cried, rolling his body into the red cap's leg. Cuthbert crashed into the nearest garden box, and Sir Justinian leapt on top of him.

"My catmint!" the fairy cried, grappling with Sir Justinian.

"Hey! Knock it off!" Shade shouted. She circled the two wrestlers but, being a wee sprite, could think of no way to separate them. "Stop, you meatheads! Stop! A little help with these nitwits, somebody?"

The Professor pulled a pitcher of ice water out of his jacket and splashed it on the two. Ginnie, for her part, ran over and screamed, "Knock it off, dummies!" Her piercing shriek made all of them drop to their knees and cover their ears in pain.

"Right hard on the throat, that is," Ginnie coughed and rubbed her neck. The Professor pulled out a lozenge and handed it to her.

"All right, you two," Shade shouted, her ears still ringing. "The next one of you who raises a fist against the other is going to have me to deal with!"

"But the fiend—"

"Didn't look like he was doing anything," Shade said.

"Yeah! *You* are the one who attacked *me* in *my* garden!"

"But you stalked the place with dread weapon in hand—"

"That sickle is a gardening tool! I was coming out to cut some flowers to decorate this old wreck and some rosemary for an herbal tea to help Fiona and me with our allergies. I mean, look at how red our eyes are."

"But your cap! It's soaked red with the blood of—"

"Raspberries. I've got a really dry, itchy scalp, and raspberry juice helps."

"There! You see?" Shade slapped Sir Justinian's shoulder.

Sir Justinian blushed. "I'm terribly sorry. I do get a bit carried away. It's just that there's an awful lot of talk of you killing people."

Ginch nodded. "Yeah, and calling you house the 'Tower of the Dead Souls' make-a you sound—"

"Actually, it's the Tower of *Dred Soulis*," Cuthbert explained. "That's the guy who built it. My great-great-grandfather bought it cheap because, well, it's on the side of a big creepy mountain."

"Oh. That no sounds-a so scary then."

"And I've never killed anyone. Grandpa Robin used to get a bit carried away, but my dad, Robin, Jr., and I have only ever tried to scare away people who tried to bother us. Now if you all are done attacking me for no reason—"

"Again, I do apologize," Sir Justinian said.

"—and quizzing me about my home, real estate holdings, and alleged history of violence, would you kindly explain exactly *why* I've been assaulted in my own garden?"

"Well, to be honest, the attack wasn't necessarily part of the plan." Shade glared at Sir Justinian. For a moment, she thought she should probably come up with a clever ruse so that she could sneak into the tower and try to find the books. Then she remembered all the times over the past several days she had attempted clever ruses. "I'm part of a secret organization called the Great Library's Unseen Guardians—"

"Wait—you're G.L.U.G.ers?" Cuthbert asked, skeptically eyeing the Professor and Ginch.

"Actually, just the sprite and me," Ginnie said. "I'm Máire Bowser's granddaughter, and she's related to Moonshadow. The others couldn't make it up here."

"Hear that, Fiona?" Cuthbert nudged the banshee, who glowered at them and whispered something none of them could make out. "Mom always said you'd come someday."

"Your mom?"

"Yeah. My mom. Alexandria. Come with me and we'll get you those books."

"Alexandria was your mother?" Shade asked as Cuthbert led them to the tower.

"Yep. Grew up near the base of the mountain. She and Dad were childhood sweethearts, so when the library fell, she came back here, married Dad, and moved into the old family home. So does this mean it's safe for books down below again? Fiona and I and the other fairies who live up here don't get around much."

Shade thought of Norwell Drabbury. "They're mostly safe. Probably as safe as they'll ever be."

"Well, that's good to hear."

The ground floor of the Tower of Dred Soulis was one immense circular room with a high, vaulted ceiling and a large, candle-covered chandelier. The walls contained two fireplaces, one clearly for cooking. Arched alcoves where light came in through cracked but very clean windows and bookcases crammed with books filled the walls. Near the cooking fire was a battered dining table on top of which sat several bottles of wine, pots of honey and jam, and platters of tea cakes, blueberry scones, and raspberry tarts. Arranged in front of the other fireplace were worn but comfortable-looking leather chairs and a small sofa on top of a colorful braided rug. In the very center of the room was a spiral staircase. "I'll just pop upstairs and get the books. Have a little bite to eat if you like. We're having a few friends over for our monthly—"

The banshee muttered something to Cuthbert that none of the rest could make out. "What do you mean the Llewellyns aren't coming?" Fiona muttered again and pointed at Sir Justinian. "He did? Then I guess it'll just be us and the Bjargmanns, then, which is too bad since Steinn hardly ever finishes the reading."

"Say, is-a Steinn the little rock guy?" Ginch asked.

"Yes. He and his wife, Crystal, are both ellyllon."

"Justinian kinda, sorta threatened to kill them too."

"Sorry," Sir Justinian offered, "but it's a mistake anyone could have made, really."

Cuthbert frowned at the troop. "So in addition to attacking me in my own garden, you have scared off every member of my book club except Fiona? Okay, wait here, touch nothing, be nice to my girlfriend, and—" he paused to glare at the Professor, who was stuffing scone after scone into his pocket, "—no snacks! I officially rescind your invitation to snack."

Cuthbert's metal shoes clanged up the steps as the Professor pouted and returned scones from his pants to the tray. The banshee eyed them warily. Everyone stood around in awkward silence.

"So . . . there's a really great library at the base of the mountain now," Shade said. "On the south face. Shaped like a big tree. Lots of books. You can borrow them. Not just you, I mean. Anyone really. But you and Cuthbert should come down sometime. The others too. The Llewellyns and the . . . what was it? The Bergsteinns?"

Fiona finally muttered something that Shade couldn't quite make out. "Uh-huh," Shade replied. "Sure."

"What did she say?" Ginnie whispered.

"No idea," Shade whispered back.

"What are you whispering about, good sprite?" Sir Justinian asked in a low voice. "Are we plotting some sort of bold stratagem involving the books?"

"No."

"'Ey, why alla you have the whisper party?" Ginch murmured.

"We're not having a whisper party," Shade muttered through gritted teeth.

"Then whatta you do?"

The banshee frowned and mumbled. The Professor smiled and gave her a thumbs-up.

"'Ey, partner, whatta she say?" Ginch whispered.

The Professor shrugged.

The banshee rolled her eyes, then moved all the food to one end of the table and began spreading out the sheet she held. Shade swatted Sir Justinian's arm. "See! I told you it was a tablecloth!"

"Here—the rarest, most important books from the Great Library." Cuthbert shoved a small wooden chest into Sir Justinian's arms. "Now I don't mean to be inhospitable, but I'd like you all to leave so I can get cleaned up, and Fiona and I can go calm down our friends and maybe salvage our book club meeting."

"Yeah. Get the donkle out, you thistlepricks," Fiona said, loud and clear enough for everyone to hear. Which they did.

27

In which our true enemy is
revealed . . .

Once they reached the bottom of the stone stairs, Shade opened the chest. Inside were six books. Two had blank, flaking leather covers barely attached to the yellowed pages coming loose between them. The other four, while old and worn, were in better condition and had writing on their covers: *The Fairy Chronicle* by Ælfrëd the Pretty

Good, *The Final Judgment Book* compiled by order of Uiliemus the Conqueror, *Codex Poetica*, and *The Muiredach Grimoire.*

Ginch tapped the cover of the grimoire. "I bet-a you this is what the Doochess of the Sighs try to get."

"Maybe." Shade took it from him. "Everybody grab a book and see what's inside."

"This is-a the book of really depressing poetry," Ginch said after a few minutes. "You gotta read the sad old sailor talking about being sad, the sad old wanderer talking about being sad, the poem about the ruins and how sad they look . . . "

"That's better than mine," Ginnie sighed. "It's just a long list of property and who owned it."

"Mine is a much more interesting read, my friends," Sir Justinian said. "'Tis a month-by-month, year-by-year history of Elfame. The beginning is dull—a lot about elections, whatever those are, and laws and trade and the like—but there are some terribly rousing accounts of battles at the end. Still, hardly seems like something worth sacking and burning a library over. How about you, my learned companion?"

The Professor held up the two untitled works to show their runic language, unknown by everyone.

"And you, fair sprite?"

"It's a book of bibliomancy." Shade flipped through *The Muiredach Grimoire*. "There are spells for creating copies of books, repairing bindings, darkening faded ink, banishing bookworms . . . It's great stuff, but I don't really see any reason why anyone other than a librarian would want—wait!" Shade stopped flipping. "I think this is it. Listen: 'Being a Spell So That the Well-Dressed Librarian Need Fear No Iron.'"

"A spell that makes fairies immune to iron?" Sir Justinian asked, his brow furrowed.

"Kind of weird wording, but yeah."

Ginnie Bowser whistled appreciatively. "I know some villains who'd pay me an arm and a leg—maybe even literally—for that." The others all glared at her. "I wouldn't *actually* sell it to them. Look, I've been a fake criminal mastermind for most of my life—these thoughts just come to me, okay?"

Sir Justinian picked up the book. "I did wonder how our new friend Cuthbert—"

"I no think he and his ghoul-friend like us," Ginch interjected.

"—could wear iron boots. This spell must be the answer. Should this fall into the wrong hands, like those of our enemy Lady Perchta, they who wield it would be nigh unstoppable. This book must be either destroyed—"

"*No.*" Shade snatched the book away and clasped it to her chest. "I watched the books I grew up with burn. I'll be donkled if I ever let another book be destroyed."

"Then it must be taken and secured someplace safe."

"We'll take it to the Grand Library." Shade gathered all of the books and stowed them in her backpack. "I doubt there's a safer place in the world."

●

For hours, down they climbed, tired but buoyed by the thought that they were almost done. Shade should have been jubilant. She had completed a generations-long family mission. She had found priceless, one-of-a-kind books, lost for more than four hundred seasons, and was bringing them to the Grand Library. And she had kept a powerful weapon out of the hands of her archenemy, Lady Perchta (she still had trouble accepting the fact that a reclusive bookworm like her had an archenemy). Yet her thoughts were troubled. *It feels like I'm missing something here, something important, but what?*

Shade hid her qualms from her companions and joined in their pleasant banter as they made their way to the base of Mount Wyrd back to the library tree.

Their jokes soon fell silent, and their smiles vanished. At the base of the tree stood Grand Scrutinizer Norwell Drabbury, torch in hand, surrounded by a score of assorted fairies—some wearing Seelie Court livery, some in that of the Sluagh, still others sporting red caps—all of them armed and spoiling for a fight. At the front near a smoldering campfire were Trudgemore and Grouse, bronze daggers held to their throats. The air was heavy with a thick, oily stench.

"Welcome back," Drabbury called out. "I trust your

expedition up Mount Wyrd was productive. No doubt you've found some excellent additions to your beloved library."

"You mean the long-lost books from the library of Alexandria?" Ginch asked.

"Exactly."

"We no find-a nothing. And I never even hear about the books of Alexandria." Ginch winked at Shade. She groaned.

Drabbury smiled a vicious, sharp-toothed smile. "Let us forego the ridiculous charade—"

The Professor sprang forward, held up three fingers, then one finger, and began to pantomime walking. "Okay, it's-a the three words," Ginch said. "First word is-a 'walk'? 'Stroll'?"

"'Go'?" suggested Ginnie, to which the Professor pointed and nodded. He held up two fingers and began making snatching motions.

"'Grab'! 'Steal'! 'Get'!" Ginch called out. The Professor nodded and tapped his nose at the last one. "I think I know. Is it 'Go get-a donkled'?"

The Professor smiled and shook his hand. "We

make-a the good team! Why we once win the Upper Swinetoe senior varsity charade tournament with—"

"Enough of this nonsense!" Drabbury roared, his eyes burning red behind his dark glasses.

"'Ey, you're the one who suggested we play the charades," Ginch objected.

"You will hand over the books," Drabbury demanded, "or we will take them from you after you have watched us kill your friends and burn your beloved library to the ground."

"Dost thou think my squire would truly prefer dishonorable surrender to an honorable death?" Sir Justinian scoffed.

"Actually, I would," Grouse grumbled. "I really, really would."

"Truly?" Sir Justinian looked stunned.

"I think I'd vote 'surrender' too, in case you're wondering," Trudgemore said.

Shade looked to the others. "What do we do? We can't let him have these books but we can't let him kill our friends."

Just then the door to the library tree opened and

Ronnie Bowser walked out with the massive troll Thornburgh and several rough-looking fairies. Ginnie gave a slight nod and wink in her direction, then whispered to the others, "That's what we do. Attack before they notice that my sister—"

"It's doon, boss," Ronnie said to Drabbury. "Ain't no blokes goin' to coom oot o' there. Now let's clean oop this mess."

"You're working with Drabbury? You traitor!" Ginnie shouted and charged at her sister. Thornburgh strode forward and swung his massive war club, striking Ginnie squarely in the stomach and sending her flying through the air to crash in front of Shade and the others. She groaned, "Why . . . would you . . . ?"

Ronnie smirked. "It's like this, sis. You know how we was playin' at being villains to protect Gran's book? Well, I actually like bein' a villain better than I like babysittin' a stupid book. So when Drabbury here cooms in an offers to help me get rid of me secretly goody-goody sis and set me oop as head crime boss o' all Elfame, well, couldn't say no, could I?"

"*You* were the rat that grassed on me in Bilgewater!" Ronnie growled as Sir Justinian helped her up.

"And you snuck off and told Snorewell Drudgery there when we went to the Hollow Hills and when we came here, didn't you, blueberry-brain?" Shade pointed an accusatory finger at her.

Ronnie smiled. "Yez was all supposed to be nicked by the bizzies at the warehouse while I handed over me book at the safe house. Then we tried to grab yez in the hills."

"In the end, I realized that it would be much easier for us if we let you do all the work of climbing Mount Wyrd and fetching the books for us." The bugbear chuckled. "Many thanks."

Ginnie stared daggers at her sister. "Gran would be ashamed of you!"

"You shoot yoor mooth aboot Gran!" Ronnie shouted, her blue face flushing a deep purple. "I'm sick to death o' hearing aboot bloody Gran! It's always 'our Gran' this and 'our Gran' that with you! Gran always did like you best! As far as I'm concerned, Gran can joost—"

Whatever Ronnie Bowser thought Gran could do was interrupted by the mighty crackle of twin lightning bolts blazing out the door of the library tree, striking several of the fairies in Drabbury's gang. They fell, twitching and smoking on the ground. Standing in the doorway was a stooped old cowlug in homespun brown clothing wearing two smoking metal gauntlets on his hands. "Oh, that did work well," he said, seemingly to himself as he looked appraisingly at them. "Precision could be improved a tad . . . "

"Poor Richard!" Shade shouted.

He looked up and smiled. "My dear Shade! I'm happy to report that I made two breakthroughs while you were out. First, these—" Poor Richard paused to blast a couple of goblins and a spriggan who had begun to charge at him. "And then Martinko's poison: *bugbear* venom. So as soon as I saw the Grand Scrutinizer and his goons marching through our beloved library, I—"

"What are you waiting for?" Drabbury roared. "Attack him, you fools!"

"We must attack as well, my comrades!" Sir Justinian cried, drawing his sword and rushing at Drabbury's thugs. "Have at thee!"

Shade, Ginch, and the Professor watched, unsure what to do, as everyone else sprang into action. More lightning bolts blasted from Poor Richard, felling Seelie and Sluagh alike. Trudgemore chomped down hard on the hand of the goblin threatening him and kicked up his back legs, sending a couple of elves flying. Ginnie Bowser gave a mighty shriek and threw herself at the crowd, punching and kicking her way toward her backstabbing sister. Grouse's reluctant battle training kicked in and he grabbed his captor's arm and flipped him forward, slamming him to the ground. Sir Justinian laughed and swung his sword in an arc that slashed through the leather armor on two of Drabbury's goons. They ran screaming away as the flesh that had touched iron sizzled.

"'Ey! Whatta you know!" Ginch elbowed Shade and pointed as the Professor pulled a bag of popcorn from his coat and began to eat. "I think we're-a gonna win!"

But the brownie's optimism was short-lived as one by one his comrades fell. Grouse ran to grab his iron skillet from beside the campfire but was tackled by a burly dwarf. Goblins swarmed Ginnie and held her in place while Ronnie grasped her sister's furry collar and delivered a vicious headbutt. Fairies piled onto Trudgemore's back, weighing him down too much for him to kick, and then a tall wulver grabbed his reins and held a short sword to his neck. As for the brave Sir Justinian, surely in a fair fight he would have prevailed, but this was no fair fight: Spear-wielding elves in Seelie Court livery encircled him, their sharp-tipped weapons holding him at bay. "Cowards and traitors all!" Sir Justinian declared, searching for an opening that did not exist.

That left only Poor Richard. His hands crackled with electricity as he looked for a clear shot that wouldn't harm any of his friends now in the clutches of their foes. In that moment of hesitation, Thornburgh snatched an ax from a nearby goblin and hurled it at the little cowlug. The ax spun end over end and buried itself in Poor Richard's chest. The blow lifted him off his feet and sent him crashing to the ground. His gauntlets sparked a few times and then fell, seemingly like their owner, dead.

"No!" Shade screamed. She, Ginch, and the Professor ran to the little cowlug and huddled around his body. His hat was gone; his eyeglasses were cracked and askew. Shade reached out to touch his face but started back when he gave a cough and reached up to fix his glasses.

"Oh, dear," he said, studying his gauntlets. "It may take days to fix—"

"You're alive!" Shade gasped. "How—?"

Poor Richard pulled open his jacket. The blade of the ax was buried in the cover of *Uncommon Nonsense*. "I told you I always keep it close to my heart. In addition to it being a lovely sentiment, I've always thought it a wise safety precaution to keep a nearly indestructible book in front of my internal organs."

"And now to make sure we have no other unnecessary interruptions . . . " Drabbury roared, then threw his torch at the library tree. There was a blinding flash of light and a blast of intense heat. Shade rubbed at her eyes. When her vision cleared, in front of her she saw the Grand Library, burning from roots to branches.

In which villains crow and fairies glow . . .

S hade stared in horror at the white flames that ate away at the library tree. "How . . . how could you . . . "

Drabbury laughed. "Quite easily. Dragon Oil. We doused the tree with it while awaiting your return."

"Thou dishonorable, dastardly dog!" Sir Justinian cried out from his circle of spear tips. "Dragon Oil has been banned from Elfame—"

"Since the Trajan-Hygelac Treaty, after which all known copies of the formula were supposedly destroyed. However, one of the perks of being Grand Scrutinizer is rooting out—and keeping for oneself—all sorts of wonderful bits of knowledge, like the formula for Dragon Oil, crop-withering spells, and so forth. You see, knowledge is power, and I mean to control all of it."

"So thou can serve as an obedient lapdog to thy lady, the Duchess of Sighs?" Sir Justinian looked almost willing to impale himself on the spears holding him at bay just to get to the bugbear.

Drabbury's lip curled up in a mocking sneer. "Perchta and a number of other discontented nobles throughout the land, both Seelie and Sluagh, may believe that I serve them—and they have been more than happy to provide me with troops to do my bidding and scholars to try to crack that blasted code of Alexandria's, which has been happening under your very noses in your own library for the past week—but in the end it is they who will serve me. Backed by the fairies I've recruited in secret and armed with the wisdom I've stolen and hoarded as Grand Scrutinizer, I will be unstoppable, especially since the one single threat to my power . . . " Drabbury pointed back toward the flaming library tree behind him, " . . . is no more."

"Well, then, the joke's on you, Grand Insquishitor!" Ginch declared. "Because that's-a no the only library tree! The Grand Library, it's-a here and-a there and-a all over the place!" The Professor grabbed a handful of peanuts out of his pocket and threw them at the bugbear while blowing a raspberry. "The Professor says, 'The nuts to you!'"

"True." The bugbear smiled. "Or it *was* true until minutes ago. You see, there are plenty of fairies in Elfame concerned with the 'corrupting' influence of books who are more than willing—eager even—to do away with every last book . . . and every library that houses them. You might be surprised at how easy it was to organize mobs to burn them all down, especially when the library, ironically, gave me and my agents immediate access to every single community with a library tree. And for the record, little sprite, the residents of Pleasant Hollow were *especially* enthusiastic about my little plan. This tree that burns behind us is the last of them, and with it dies the Grand Library and all the books and book lovers it housed."

Shade stood in stunned silence. *My home! My books! Destroyed . . . burned . . . again!* she thought. But this was worse, she realized, as tears rolled down her face. Because this time it wasn't just a home and it wasn't just books—this time it was also her *friends*. François, Émilie, Johannes, Caxton, Dewey—all of them and who knows how many visitors had been inside. And now they were gone.

Like water in a teakettle, Shade felt rage bubble up within her until it finally boiled over. Screaming in fury, she flew at the mighty bugbear. What she hoped to accomplish, who can say—probably not even her. Drabbury, much more swiftly and adeptly than one might expect of a fairy his size, swatted her to the ground. Shade lay gasping for breath in the dirt but only for a moment. Drabbury yanked her up, slit the straps on her backpack, and tossed her over to Ginch and the Professor.

Drabbury opened the backpack and smiled. "Thank you, my dear, for so kindly delivering to me the— here! It's here! The book that will bring down kingdoms!"

The bugbear pulled out *The Muiredach Grimoire* and threw off his glasses to reveal multifaceted bee eyes, red and blazing like two large rubies with fires burning at their cores. Feverishly, he flipped through the spellbook, grinning in maniacal glee. "I have it! Gather round, my loyal subjects! Gather round and we will be freed of our greatest weakness!"

"Trying to hit an inside straight when playing Slap-a-the-Selkie?" Ginch offered.

"Iron. With this spell, we and all who join us will be immune. Then we shall take up arms forged from the cursed metal and cut a bloody swath through all who oppose us!"

"No!" Justinian lunged at the spearmen between him and Drabbury, but those behind him swept his feet out from under him. The troops piled on and disarmed him, although one fox-faced goblin ran away screaming and flailing at the burning cut on his arm that he earned for his troubles.

"What you have witnessed, you need never fear again," Drabbury declared, pointing at the panicking goblin. He then looked down at the book and began chanting in his deep, growly voice the words—unknown and possibly unknowable to all who heard them—on the page.

"We've got to stop him!" Shade cried. "He can't make these thistlepricks ironproof!"

"'Ey, booger-the-bear!" Ginch shouted at him. "You gotta the untied shoe! And there's-a the toilet paper stuck to you foot!"

The Professor took out a straw and a handful of peas and started shooting them at Drabbury's face.

"Your mother was a honey thief and your father licked salmon!" Shade called out.

Their efforts, however, were in vain. The Grand Scrutinizer continued unabated, his chanting growing more and more vehement and his bug eyes burning brighter and brighter until at last, flecks of spittle flying from his maw, he howled: "Klaatu Barada NIKTO!"

That final word echoed, then all was quiet except for the crackle of flames. And then everyone there began to glow. Shade could feel her skin getting warm and tingling . . . but not the skin on her face and hands. She looked down at herself, then around at everyone else. *Only our clothes are glowing*, she realized. Suddenly, the wrinkles and folds in her clothes straightened out and the yellow glow faded. *'Being a Spell So That the Well-Dressed Librarian Need Fear No Iron'. . . Now I think I get it!*

29

In which the importance of close
reading is demonstrated . . .

Drabbury gave a triumphant roar. "It is done!
Now we are unbeatable!"

"I bet I can beat you, Drudgery," Shade
jeered. "You and all your rock-headed, grub-chewing
goons."

Drabbury snorted. "I believe, you impertinent little
insect, that you are long overdue a lesson in respecting
your betters."

"Haven't met any yet, fuzzbutt."

"Here, boss, let me," the massive troll Thornburgh said. He cracked the knuckles of his long, sharp-nailed fingers. "This oughta be good for a laugh. And I can't even remember the last time I ate sprite meat. It's like quail but buggier."

"'Ey, little Sprootshade—whatta you do?" Ginch's brow furrowed with concern. "You gotta the death wish?"

"No. I think I know what I'm doing." Shade turned to the Professor. "I need gloves. Please tell me you have gloves."

The Professor rummaged through his various pockets. Eventually, he pulled out bronze gauntlets with one hand and canvas gardening gloves with the other. Shade took the gardening gloves. "Okay, let's hope this works."

Shade walked toward the troll, picking up Grouse's iron skillet as she went. She gripped it with both hands and held it over one shoulder like a baseball bat. Thornburgh tossed back his head and laughed. "Okay, bug girl! Okay! Tell you what—I'll give you one shot. One free shot because this . . . this is just too funny!"

Thornburgh held his long, long arms out to either side and strode forward, eliciting delighted laughter and cheers from Drabbury's minions. He stopped in front of Shade, towering over her, guffawing heartily. Shade made a silent prayer to St. Eeyore, then leapt up and swung the skillet, smacking the savage troll right on his filthy, bare belly. Thornburgh's laughter abruptly ceased. Confusion and panic filled his eyes as he looked down at the red, slightly smoking circle on his stomach. He let out a roar of pain that silenced his laughing comrades, and he clutched and clawed at his burning belly. Shade, heartened by this, smashed the skillet down on the toes of both of his shoeless feet, making him dance about in pain.

"Grouse! Catch." Shade tossed him the skillet. Of course, since she was a bookish sprite unaccustomed to athletic activities, her throw was off and the skillet hit the jaw of the dwarf who was holding him, which proved to be effective enough. The dwarf grabbed his now burning jaw as Grouse swept up the skillet and struck every patch of bare fairy flesh near him. Meanwhile, the Professor donned his bronze gauntlets, grabbed an iron pot from Grouse's cooking supplies, and bounded through the crowd, clonking fairy after fairy on the head. Ginnie Bowser, meanwhile, broke free from her captors and tackled Ronnie to the ground where the two grappled, and Trudgemore kicked and bit at every fairy around him.

And of course, there was the brave, noble Sir Justinian. With a swashing blow, he knocked aside the elfin spearmen standing between him and Drabbury. "Have at thee, thou blackguardly bugbear!" he cried as he charged. He swung his sword, but the bugbear blocked the blow with his two long elbow barbs. The places where the sword touched the stingers sizzled, but if it pained Drabbury, he took no notice as he slashed with claw and barb at the noble knight, who was forced to give ground because of the great hulking bulk of the bugbear but who, hero that he was, refused to yield.

Shade glanced about the melee, trying to figure out something she could do, when the head of a mace came swinging directly at her face. She gave a yelp and closed her eyes. She felt herself be yanked backward and opened her eyes to see Ginch dragging her by her coat away from the crowd. "Whatta you do, little Sprootshade! You wanna get smooshed? I say we let the fighters do the fighting."

"But we've got to do *something*! They're outnumbered! There's no way they'll survive without help!"

Suddenly there was a loud clanging—it was Cuthbert, racing their way with a swirling cloud of gray smoke by his side. "Now that's-a what I call the good timing!" Ginch said, as Cuthbert vaulted over them feet first to kick a pair of goblins directly in the faces, and Fiona the banshee materialized in front of a swollen spriggan and gave a hideous shriek that left the fairy writhing on the ground, clutching his ears.

Shade watched the battle roil in front her. The appearance of Cuthbert, the most feared fairy in all of Elfame, made some of Drabbury's troops break ranks and flee, but most stayed and fought. Shade wracked her brains for something, anything, she could do to help. Suddenly, a mighty crack sounded and the flaming library tree toppled, every branch and leaf consumed by white flame. Despair filled her heart. But then a vague memory floated up in her mind and kindled the faintest flickering flame of hope. "Professor!" she called. "Professor! Get over here!"

The pixie sprang through the air and landed in front of her, saluting as he landed. His gauntleted hand clonked against his forehead and he staggered back, shaking his head.

Shade grabbed the lapels of his coat and pulled him to her. "You tried to eat some Grand Library acorns and then shoved them into your pocket. Do you still have them?"

The Professor's eyes lit up and he began to search his pockets. He tossed handful after handful out—scones, wedges of cheese, silverware, cups, spools of thread, hammers, hats, wigs, fake mustaches, coins, jewelry, a rubber chicken, a real live chicken, a confused-looking

Will o' the Wisp, and lots of hard-boiled eggs—until finally he triumphantly held up a single acorn. Shade snatched it from him.

"If all the trees are gone, could everybody still be alive somehow?" she asked. The Professor scratched his head and shrugged. "We'll just have to hope."

Shade dug a hole in the dirt with her heel and dropped the acorn in. The ground shook and buckled. Shade ran hand-in-hand-in-hand with Ginch and the Professor as a mighty oak erupted from the ground, launching the fairies nearest it into the air. In a matter of moments, a new library tree loomed large at the base of Mount Wyrd. Shade gave a cry of joy as the door in its side was flung open and Yaxley and Ront strode out, paused a moment as they surveyed the brawl in front of them, and then threw themselves into it, fists flying. Right on their heels was Émilie, her serene marble face now a study in fury. Just behind her François paused in the doorway, looking around at the vast outdoors with anxiety, placed his hand on his chest, and took a couple deep breaths. He then grabbed a pair of elves by their Seelie Court tabards, soared into the air on great granite wings, and dropped them to the ground.

One by one Drabbury's fairies either fell or fled, while there, at the center of the battle, Sir Justinian remained locked in mortal combat with the Grand Scrutinizer. The valiant knight stabbed and slashed as he ducked sweeping claws, dodged snapping jaws, and parried jabbing stingers. Stepping back to avoid an especially close swipe, Justinian tripped on an unconscious goblin and fell. The bugbear seized the opportunity and stabbed downward with his elbow, burying it deep in the fair knight's shoulder. Betraying not the slightest bit of pain, Justinian slashed the barb off at the elbow. Drabbury howled in pain. Justinian hauled back his sword arm and cracked Drabbury on the side of the head with the pommel of the sword. The bugbear's eyes rolled back in his head and he toppled over, unconscious, next to the brave knight.

Seeing their leader fall took the fight out of the remaining members of Drabbury's crew, who either dropped their weapons and surrendered or fled. Sir Justinian slowly rose to his feet. He grasped the barb in his shoulder and grimaced as he wrenched it free and dropped it to the ground. He smiled as he staggered toward Shade. "The day . . . verily . . . is ours . . . " he panted.

Then his knees buckled, and he collapsed at her feet.

30

𝒥n which the author jolly well
better not kill off the only properly
heroic character in this dratted book
if he knows what's good for him!

S hade, Ginch, and the Professor crowded around
Sir Justinian. "Get back," commanded Grouse
as he pushed through them and knelt next to
Sir Justinian. He helped his master sit up, his arm
around the knight's shoulder.

Sir Justinian grimaced. "Argh! . . . feels like my veins are filled with molten lead . . . "

Shade scanned the ground until she found the severed bugbear stinger. She ran to Poor Richard. "Here! You've got to use this to make an antidote!"

Poor Richard shook his head sadly. "I wish I could, but I don't know how. It's never been done before."

"You have to try!"

"Even if I succeeded," Poor Richard lowered his voice, "our good knight wouldn't live long enough. Martinko hovers on death's door from just a slight scratch from one of those stingers—"

"Martinko! That's it! We'll cast a stasis spell and—"

Poor Richard put a hand on Shade's shoulder. "With the amount of venom in his system, even a stasis spell wouldn't buy us enough time. He has mere minutes to live."

Grouse gazed down at Sir Justinian and brushed his graying hair from his feverish brow. "It's okay. You'll be okay. Tomorrow, I'll cook up a good breakfast, and you'll drone on, as you always do, about some stupid, boring 'noble battle' and . . . "

"No, good Grouse, no . . . " Sir Justinian closed his eyes and smiled. "My devoted squire . . . "

"I wasn't that devoted. In fact—"

"And my boon companions—"

The Professor pulled an inflated balloon out of his coat that Ginch instantly popped. "He said 'boon,' not 'balloon.' We've been through this before, paisan."

"Every warrior's journey . . . " Sir Justinian continued, undeterred, " . . . must one day lead to death . . . that undiscovered country . . . from whose bourn no traveler returns . . . Today, I have come to the end of my journey . . . Thus begins my eternal rest. But it is a sweet one, my good friends . . . knowing that I leave behind my squire—a noble, skilled, and devout warrior—worthy to carry on my fight . . . " All of the fairies exchanged doubtful looks and turned to Grouse, whose tear-filled eyes remained fixed on the dying knight. " . . . and so many friends of stout hearts, strong arms, and good cheer . . . O good Grouse . . . if thou didst ever hold me in thy heart . . . throughout this harsh world . . . tell my story."

"I will, sir," Grouse sobbed. "I will."

Sir Justinian sighed contentedly. "Good. Good, my squire," he said, his voice fading. "I have but one last thing to say . . . and the rest is silence . . . "

Everyone crowded close to hear his last words and witness his final moments. But instead of the sort of heartbreaking, inspiring, morally improving final utterance that any decent, self-respecting tale of heroism would give us, there was instead the horrid hawking of someone clearing a phlegmy throat, followed by the wet splat of spittle striking our tragic hero. Everyone looked up in outrage to see who was responsible.

"That oughta do it," Trudgemore said.

"What the donkle are you doing?" Shade screamed.

"Fatcha-coota-matchca, mule!" Ginch made a rude gesture.

"Unicorn," Trudgemore replied coolly. "I'm a unicorn."

"The dingle-dangle you are!" Ginnie objected. "You haven't got a horn, you jerk!"

"In my heart I do."

"You are a mule!" Shade yelled, jabbing her finger in Trudgemore's face. "You are a dingle-dangle mule, and a horrid, stupid, cruel one because you have just ruined the last moments—"

"They're not his last—"

"Shut up, mule! You have ruined his final—"

"But they're not his final—"

"SHUT UP! Poor Sir Justinian, the most brave and noble—"

"And they call mules stubborn." Trudgemore butted Shade hard, sending her with a whomp onto her backside. "Just be quiet a second and look."

Shade looked down to see a yellow, blood-streaked ichor flow from Justinian's wound. When the last of it oozed out, the hole closed shut without even a scar. Justinian's eyes flew open, and he gasped great lungfuls of air.

"Sir! You're alive!" Grouse cried.

Sir Justinian's breathing slowed. "Yes. By St. Figgymigg, I live! 'Twould appear this noble beast has saved my life!"

"But how—?" Shade began.

"Unicorn spit," Trudgemore said. "Told you it cured poison."

"Ha-ha!" Ginch clapped his hands. "Say, you really are the mulicorn!"

"That's 'unicorn,' but you're gettin' there. We're just gonna have to keep workin' on you," Trudgemore said hopefully.

"Release me, you curs!" barked Grand Scrutinizer Drabbury, who had awakened to find his hands and feet bound.

"We'll leave that, if they so choose, to officials of the Seelie Court and the Sluagh Horde," Émilie said.

"'Oo, I zink, will be very, very interested to 'ear about your actions today," added François, as he glanced longingly back at the door to the library and nervously up at the skies.

"And thy plans to conquer Elfame, villain," Sir Justinian said as Grouse helped him stand.

The bugbear laughed. "With my influence and connections? Who do you think would possibly take your word over mine?"

"I for one!" declared the black-cloaked elfin boy as he stepped out of the crowd of scholars and patrons who had been trapped in the Grand Library. He threw back his hood to reveal his dark, handsome face. "You know who I am, do you not, Grand Scrutinizer?"

"I know you, whelp," Drabbury growled. "And you forget—I have supporters amongst *both* the Seelie and the Sluagh."

The green-clad elfin girl came forward and removed *her* hood, revealing shimmering white hair streaked with bright purple. "I don't know how many supporters you'll have when it becomes known that both the heir to the Sluagh throne and the daughter of the late Seelie king and queen were almost killed by your actions today."

Drabbury's eyes burned. "You think two children can stop me?"

"Two royal children who love books and know how important it is that all fairies have access to them?" the Seelie princess smirked. "Frankly, yes."

"Books for all fairies?" the bugbear spat. "You really think all of them should read? Books, knowledge— they belong to those with the strength and the vision to rule. Give books to the commoners and it will fill their heads with ideas, and those, you silly little fools, are far more dangerous than any weapon. But do not doubt for one second that I, Norwell Drabbury, won't someday—mmff, mmff, mmff!"

What Norwell Drabbury would someday do was cut off by the Professor stuffing a pair of filthy socks in his mouth. "The Professor says to put-a the sock in it," Ginch explained. "Hey partner, how long since you wash those socks?" The Professor held up two fingers. "Two weeks?" The Professor shook his head. "Two months?" The Professor shook his head. "Two years?" The Professor nodded. "Ey, mulicorn, you might need to spit on the booger-the-bear later."

"*Unicorn*. And he can take his chances," Trudgemore snorted.

"My servants and I will take Drabbury to Ande-Dubnos and hold him until we can make arrangements for a hearing and trial," the Sluagh prince announced.

"Why not take him to Dinas Ffaraon, Prince Beow? I believe we Seelie can do just as good of a job imprisoning the bugbear—probably better, in fact—as you Sluagh," the Seelie princess said.

"First, I doubt you have anything nearly as secure as our royal dungeons, Princess Viola. Second, Dinas Ffaraon is at least three times as far from here as Ande-Dubnos, and in case you haven't noticed, this is the only library tree left. We can't just walk out a doorway and be home anymore."

There was a collective groan, then assorted grumbles, amongst the assorted fairies and humans who had gathered outside the library tree. "It'll take weeks to get home!" "My husband and kids will be so worried!" "Who's going to take the varg out for walkies?" "Eh, never did much care for the place—guess I'll be mountain folk now."

"Hang on," said Shade. "We're smart people." She glanced at Ginch and the Professor, who waved enthusiastically. "Mostly. And we've got the largest collection of books in history at our disposal. I'm sure that someone here can figure out a reasonably fast way to get everyone home."

The crowd nodded and murmured its approval of the plan. Then everyone began to scratch their heads, stroke their beards, or tap their fingers on their teeth in thought. After a few quiet moments, a tall human wizard dressed all in gray muttered, "I suppose we could . . . but no, nobody would want to . . . "

"What?" Shade asked.

"Well, I know a spell that could summon giant eagles down from the mountains to give people rides home and—"

"And each one could plant a library tree and everyone else could just walk right out of the library to get home!" Shade said. "Brilliant!"

"I suppose, but I'm sure nobody would be interested in that." The wizard sighed.

"Why would anyone not want to ride on the back of a giant eagle and save themselves days or even weeks of long, exhausting travel?"

The wizard shrugged. "I don't know. Don't you think walking the whole way would be more dramatic?"

"What could be more dramatic than swooping in on the back of a giant eagle? Just summon the dingle-dangle birds!" Shade smacked the wizard's pipe to the ground. "And no smoking around the library!"

31

In which a new acronym is born . . .

Within hours, most of the library trees had been replanted, and all of the patrons had returned home. Though weakened by his near-fatal poisoning, Sir Justinian insisted on accompanying Princess Viola back to the Seelie Court with a slightly less grumbly Grouse in tow. With the library emptied out and Martinko recovering quietly after a dose of unicorn spit, the staff of the Grand Library, several G.L.U.G.ers, two bodyguards, a pair of mountain fairies, a hornless unicorn, and Shade and her friends drank coffee, hot chocolate, tea, and other beverages together in one of the reading lounges. Alexandria's books were arranged on a coffee table for all to see.

"It's not that I'm invulnerable to iron," Cuthbert explained, lifting up an ironclad foot. "I just wear heavy socks. The shoes are for this family foot condition I've got."

"If you're hurt by the iron, then how do you take the shoes on and off?" Dewey asked.

"Carefully. Very carefully."

"'Ey, little Sprootshade—how'd you figure out the iron spell was-a the dud?" Ginch asked.

"No, it did work." Shade paused to sip her cocoa. "It just wasn't the spell we all thought it was. See, I thought it was weird that a book of library spells would have a spell to make you immune to iron. Plus there was that bit about 'the well-dressed librarian.' Then when Drabbury finally cast the spell, our clothes glowed but not our skin. And when I saw all the wrinkles in my clothes straighten out, I realized it was a clothes dewrinkling spell—"

"So that a librarian need not fear burning themselves on a hot iron," Émilie finished.

"Or scorching zeir clothes." François unbuttoned his vest to reveal a triangular yellow patch on his shirt. "Well, I for one more zan welcome zis book to our collection."

"But it's not exactly the sort of book that could bring down a kingdom, is it?" Shade frowned.

"That's not the dangerous book. That one is." Cuthbert pointed at *The Fairy Chronicle*.

Everyone looked at one another. "You've read these books?" Shade asked.

"I live on a mountain. I've read every book in that tower about a hundred times."

"I am not understanding vhy a history book vould be dangerous," Johannes said.

"Oh, I don't know," Poor Richard chimed in. "You'd

be surprised by how much power comes from knowing your history."

Cuthbert nodded. "Anybody want to tell us how the Seelie Court ended up ruling the lands of fairy until the most recent war?"

"They always have," Shade replied. "When the creator made the fairies and the fairy lands, she appointed the elves of the Seelie Court as its rulers and protectors. Everybody knows that."

"Actually, not everybody knows that," Émilie said. "We have Sluagh-authored books here that claim *they* were the original rulers, betrayed and cast out by some of their own people who then established themselves as the Seelie Court."

Cuthbert snorted. "And both stories are loads of mule dung. No offense, Trudgemore."

"None taken. I'm a unicorn."

"See," Cuthbert went on, "*The Fairy Chronicle*, one of the oldest books in existence, is a year-by-year account of what happened in Elfame. If you read it, you'll learn that Elfame was originally a commonwealth with an elected government until a group of wealthy elves decided it would be better if they called the shots, so they overthrew the government and set themselves up as the new rulers. *The Final Judgment Book*'s a big list of who got what when they carved up the land after they took over. And, of course, as soon as they were in charge, those rich elves started fighting amongst themselves—"

"And the Sluagh lost and got kicked out, and the Seelie became the rulers," Shade finished.

Cuthbert nodded. "It's all in the book, along with reports of their attempts to erase all records of anything before Seelie rule—book burnings, imprisonment of former government officials, the destruction of the former site of the government, which is what the ruins on the edge of Stormfield used to be."

"Truly?" François looked amazed. "Ze nature of ze ruins has always been a great mystery."

"So all this Seelie and Sluagh stuff about 'oo's got the right to rule's just a bunch o' rubbish?" Caxton drained his mug of mead and plunked it down. "Can't imagine them nobles'll be 'appy to read any o' that!"

"They definitely won't." Ginny Bowser looked grim. "Listen, in my time as a fake crime lord, I've had a lot of dealings with members of the Court and the Horde. If word of this book gets out, they'll destroy it and anything and anyone that gets in their way. You can't keep it here."

François set his coffee down with a clatter. "I am a librarian, Mademoiselle Bowser! I 'ave devoted my life to bringing ze light of knowledge to ze world. I would razzer die zan 'ide a single book from ze people or let it be destroyed!"

"Maybe there's another way . . ." Shade said slowly. "Cuthbert, have you ever used the book-copying spell in the grimoire?"

Cuthbert nodded. "Made at least one copy of every book I have in case of mishap. More for some—can't really have a book club if everybody doesn't have a book to read. Takes quite a while, but it's a lot faster than hand-copying them."

"What if we made copies of *The Fairy Chronicle* and somehow made them secretly available without keeping an actual copy here in the library?"

Johannes took his glasses off and cleaned them meditatively with a napkin. "But I am vondering how a few secret copies of this book vill make it available to everyone like having it in our library vould."

"Oh, I think we can manage more than a few copies," Poor Richard chuckled. "One of the inventions I was working on before my home rather unfortunately exploded is a machine designed to make multiple copies of books at a fast rate. Instead of a scribe taking months or years to make one copy of a book, this machine—which I believe I could have up and running soon, especially with the help of that great-nephew of Grigor's you told me about—could make at least a hundred in a month."

Ginnie grinned. "And with my knowledge of smuggling, black markets, and secret criminal organizations, I'm sure I can get copies out to interested parties, especially if my helpers and I can use this library to get here, there, and everywhere. What do think, Yax? Ront?"

The human and the spriggan both smiled. "And 'ere

we was afraid we'd 'ave to go straight-straight now," Ront said.

"Yeah," Yaxley added. "We definitely prefer bein' crooked-straight. We's in, boss."

"And if you're looking for an out-of-the-way place to do your printing, why not set up shop in my tower?" Cuthbert offered. Fiona muttered something indistinct, although Shade was pretty sure she heard "thistlepricks" somewhere in it. "It'll be fine, Fiona. Plus, seems like a good excuse for me to finally move in with you."

Poor Richard clapped his hands together. "That would appear to settle things, then! We're done guarding the knowledge of the past—now we spread it in secret. The Great Library's Unseen Guardians are dead. Long live Book Lovers, Active and Hush-hush!"

"Wait—B.L.A.H.?" Shade said. "Can't we do better than—"

"Long Live B.L.A.H.!" everyone else cheered.

"No, apparently we cannot do better," Shade sighed.

32

In which Shade once more
reluctantly goes home . . .

hiefainess Sungleam Flutterglide fluttered
(but did not, however, glide) above the burnt
ground so that all the residents of Pleasant
Hollow could see her. The hollow that day did not
look terribly pleasant, what with more than a quarter
either reduced to ash or heavily damaged by the previous night's fire, nor did the majority of its residents,
who glared at their leader.

"Just think," the chieftainess declared cheerily, her usual smile looking rather strained, "rebuilding all of these homes—beginning with my own, of course—will be the Grandest Project in the history of Grand Projects!"

She paused to allow time for the assembled sprites to cheer. Instead, there was a great deal of unhappy mutterings and grumblings in response. "Doesn't sound that grand to me." "Build you a house right next to my Aunt Fannyfeather." "Got your Grand Project right here!"

"But the most important thing to keep in mind is that thanks to me, the council of elders, and a number of concerned citizens, we are rid of that horrible book tree, its corrupting influence, and all the unpleasant non-sprites it was attracting to our dear, dear Pleasant Hollow!"

Again, the crowd's only response was mumbled hostility. "I'd rather have the dingle-dangle tree." "Books didn't do any harm that I could see." "None of the fairies that came for the library ever even tried to burn down my house."

The chieftainess frowned, unaccustomed to anything less than enthusiastic support. "Be at ease, my fellow sprites, for we will rebuild." She raised her face and hands to the skies above. "And Pleasant Hollow will be even more pleasant and safe than it has ever—AAAGH!"

Sungleam Flutterglide streaked into the trees. The rest of the sprites looked up to see a gigantic eagle swooping down, vicious talons extended. The air was filled with the screams and flutterings of fleeing fairies. The clearing emptied. As the sprites peered out from the relative safety of the trees, Shade hopped down from the mighty raptor's back. "Again, I ask: Why would anyone not travel on the back of a giant eagle?" Shade gave the eagle a pat on the wing. "Thanks, Gwaihir."

The eagle screeched, flapped its mighty wings, and flew away. Shade reached into a pocket of her traveling coat and took out an acorn. Surveying the devastation that fire had wrought upon the village, she shook her head in disbelief and dug a hole in the ground with her boot.

"Oh, no, you don't!" Chieftainess Flutterglide flew out and landed in front of Shade. The other sprites slowly came out of hiding to watch. "You will not plant that acorn anywhere near Pleasant Hollow! Can't you see that . . . that . . . *library* has done enough damage?"

Shade snorted. "Looks more like *you* did enough damage here. Let me guess—the Grand Scrutinizer didn't bother to tell you that burning the biggest tree in the forest would cause more to burn down?"

"I'm . . . I'm sure it just slipped his mind. Besides, I believe it was the books more than the flames themselves that caused most of the damage."

"And we've hit a new level of stupid." Shade sighed. "When I replant this, maybe try reading a few books. Reading really is one of the best remedies for stupidity."

The chieftainess grabbed Shade by the wrist before she could drop the acorn. "You will not barge in here and plant a library in the middle of Pleasant Hollow against our wishes again! I forbid it!"

Shade opened her mouth to say something insulting but stopped. "You know, you might be right."

"Of course I'm right," Flutterglide huffed. "I'm the chieftainess!"

"Being in charge doesn't prove you're right. If anything, it usually proves the opposite. But in this case, you actually have a point." Shade turned to the rest of the sprites. "Last time I did this, the chieftainess and council of elders all told me not to create a library here, and I didn't listen. Today, I'm going to listen . . . to *all* of you. How many of you want the library tree back? Hands up high."

At first the sprites just stood there, blinking and looking uneasily at one another. Shade's heart fell. Then one young sprite slowly raised her hand. After a moment, another young sprite did the same. Then one of the older sprites joined them. Following their lead, sprite after sprite raised their hands until more than half the village stood with hands held high.

Shade smiled. "Well, I guess that decides that!"

"It does not!" Chieftainess Flutterglide shouted.

"The council of elders and I are in charge here—"

"For now," interrupted Shade.

"—and *we* are the ones who decide what is best for everyone!"

"I think that needs to change," Shade said, dropping the acorn in the hole. "It's high time that every fairy had some say in what's best for them. It's a really old idea, but once it makes its way back out into the world, I believe it'll spread and grow as fast as this acorn here."

With that, Shade kicked dirt onto the acorn and took several steps back, looking quite pleased with what she had done. And she wasn't the only one.

· EPILOGUE ·

*In which your humble narrator
receives truly dreadful news . . .*

As a very well read and knowledgeable Reader, I'm sure you expected that last chapter to conclude with "And they all lived happily ever after!" just as I'm sure you expected the same of our previous adventure of Shade. And if either of these books were *proper* fairy books, they would have. However, as I have made abundantly clear many times, these are *dreadful* ones. Still, I did my best to make the case to that horrid old contrarian Mr. Etter that this terrible tale should at least have a traditional ending. But as before, he would have none of it.

"Very well," I sighed after listening to him pontificate at exhaustive length about the fleeting nature of happiness. "I'll just put down 'The End' and wash my hands of the whole dratted—"

"Nope. Sorry." He had a wicked gleam in his eye. "You can't do that."

"Oh, I jolly well can!" I objected. (I must confess that I lost my temper just then, but how can one not when being forced to deal with Mr. Etter?) "The book's done, is it not?"

"Yeah, but it's not the end." Mr. Etter looked especially smug, even for him. "I mean there's a book that could undermine the power of the Seelie Court and the Sluagh Horde, a group of fairies plotting to distribute it secretly, and, of course, Sir Justinian—"

"You will not sully the one decent, noble, and inspiring character in your otherwise indecent, ignoble, and thoroughly uninspiring works by dragging him into this," I told him firmly.

"Fine. But the fact remains that there are clearly things going on in the story that have definitely *not* come to an end, which is good since we've got another book to do."

"We what?"

"Read your contract. The publisher wants three books from us."

"Good gracious, why?"

Mr. Etter shrugged. "No idea. Maybe the honor of having you narrate more of their books." He obviously meant that in jest, but it's the only explanation that makes a bit of sense. "If it makes you feel better, you could say it's the end for now."

Sadly, he's right. I am, it appears, stuck narrating yet another dreadful fairy book. I have asked my narrators union shop steward, MacKenzie "Blinky" Blinkerton, to see if there's any way to get out of it, but old Blinky assures me there is no hope. And so, until next time . . . sigh . . . I suppose I must say that this is

The End . . . for Now

· ABOUT JON ETTER ·
(written by Quentin Q. Quacksworth, Esq.)

Jon Etter was born and raised (one assumes in a barn, judging by his manners) and still lives in that vast middle part of America that holds little interest to those of us in the civilized world, although its natives seem to tolerate it well enough. As a father of two and high school English teacher, one would think him capable of being more than the subpar scribbler of silly stories that he is, although I do believe he is improving slightly. You may visit him online at www.jonetter.com if you engage in such activities.

· ABOUT QUENTIN Q. ·
QUACKSWORTH, ESQ.
(written by Jon Etter)

Quentin Q. Quacksworth has been a professional narrator for a long time—too long, some of us would argue—and has narrated many "proper" and "morally improving" books, including *Honest Jim and the Do-Right Lads*, for which he somehow won a Blabby Award for Narratorial Excellence. Feel free to ask him about it or just talk to him for five minutes, and he'll find a way to bring it up. He refuses to have anything to do with "electronic mail" or "the interwebs," so contact him via, I don't know, messenger pigeon or something.

· ABOUT ADAM HORSEPOOL ·

Adam Horsepool is an illustrator and animator living and working in Nottingham, UK. His favorite children's book (besides this dreadful series) is *Fantastic Mr. Fox* by Roald Dahl, and his favorite illustrator is Ryan Lang. To see more of Adam's art, visit him on Instagram @adam_horsepool.